The Burning

By Richard Snow

Originally published by Doubleday & Company, Inc.

September 3, 1894

One of the gravediggers squinted into the low sun. "Here comes another one."

Frank Webber looked down the hill and saw the wagon.

"Start a new trench."

"We got room for a few more in this one." The gravedigger rubbed his face with a bright blue bandanna the size of a tablecloth.

Webber watched the wagon working its way uphill, "There's more than a few coming in."

The gravedigger shrugged. "I'll tell the boys," he said; "they'll be glad for the exercise."

Webber looked at the man. "That meant to be a joke?"

The gravedigger walked away, dragging his shovel behind him through the ashes. Heat devils rose around the clean, dull metal of the blade. The man spoke briefly to five other men with shovels. One of them pulled a bottle out of his back pocket, and they passed it around.

Webber looked away. He was a temperance man--drank only milk himself-and normally he wouldn't let his men drink spirits on a job. But he'd had trouble even finding men for this job, and those he found wouldn't do it without liquor. Well, he could understand that.

The gravediggers started filling in the open trench. They had been idle for the past couple of hours, but the carpenters had been busy for a full day now, so that Webber noticed the noise of their sawing and hammering only when they stopped for meals.

The day before, Webber had ridden the train out from Pine City with the carpenters and gravediggers. The coach had been sweet with the smell of the five thousand board feet of freshly cut pine on the flat-car behind. It was a smell Webber had always loved, and would detest for the rest of his life.

The wagon reached the crest of the hill and stopped, the mule apparently stupefied by the heat. The driver, a big man with a face so streaked by ash that his features seemed blurred, sagged on the seat, elbows on his knees, hands holding loosely to the reins.

"How many?" asked Webber.

"Six, from over in the swamp."

"Many more out there?"

"Oh, Jesus, yes. There's hundreds."

Webber called to the gravediggers. "Two of you! Over here!"

After some argument two men left the trench and came over. "Better start getting these unloaded," said Webber. The men lifted down a gray corpse and put it into a coffin.

The coroner's assistant examined the corpse, pried off some jewelry, and put it in a pouch. He was a chunky man named Styles, whom the carnage seemed to have affected chiefly by reminding him of the vast injustice done when he had been passed over for coroner. "There's just no accounting for it," he had told Webber a good two dozen times. "That goddamn Cowan doesn't know the first goddamn thing about being a coroner."

Styles straightened up from the coffin and wrote in a notebook, "Unknown-Female: age about 35; dark hair; plain gold earrings; height 5.2; wore low gaiter shoes, 2 plain gold rings on finger right hand; found in swamp, one-half mile north of Hinckley."

The gravediggers lifted down a huddled corpse. "It's a little girl," said one of them. "Look, she was praying."

"You don't know that," said Styles. "Let me see her."

September 3

Webber worked for three days straight. When he got home, his wife put out some cold chicken and biscuits for him, but he had no stomach for food. He drank a glass of milk, then went into the kitchen and took down a dusty bottle of medicinal brandy, nearly full, brought it into the parlor, and finished it in an hour, while his wife watched with dismay.

He was sick in bed all the next day and didn't take a decent meal for two days after that.

August 31, 1894

It was all forest north of Minneapolis. In the southern part of the state there was nothing to draw a lumberman, but upcountry stood white pine, the perfect tree. The pines averaged out at 140 feet tall; some reached 200. Their wood was sweet and clean, and so straight-grained that a good jack could cut a board right off the log with his broadax.

Those were big days of Minnesota, and it was white pine that made them big. Settlers on the treeless prairies to the west wanted lumber for their houses, and Minnesota gave it to them, more than a billion board feet a year.

Minneapolis was a lumber town. It was also a grain town, grinding wheat into seven million barrels of flour annually. The city fed on itself, built on itself. Its perpetually muddy streets were lined with seventy miles of wooden sidewalks; one hundred and sixty thousand citizens trudged about their business on the finest lumber in the world.

The sawmills, the flour mills were the heart of the state; the railroads were its arteries. The flour men had laid track farther and farther out until just last year the city—and its lusty twin, St. Paul—hooked up with Jim Hill's Great Northern; now it could send its lumber and flour all the way to the Pacific.

One hundred and fifty miles to the north, Duluth was coming to life on the shores of Lake Superior. Iron ore in the Mesabi Range had given it the spur. For years the city had been so ugly and ambitious that it was a joke in a nation of ugly, ambitious cities. Now it was on the way to becoming a great port town, built on a hill just like San Francisco, and full of the same insular pride.

Two railroads joined the cities. Angling down from the north, they crossed almost exactly halfway between St. Paul and Duluth, and a wedge-shaped town had grown up in the northern quadrant of their joining. Hinckley.

The railroad had left Hinckley behind when it passed through in 1869, and though the town had been incorporated only since 1885, it had grown to be a regular little city of fifteen hundred inhabitants, most of them sanguine enough to believe that in a decade or so their town would be able to give Duluth a run for its money. After all, Hinckley had the Brennan Lumber Company—a monster operation employing three hundred citizens and turning out two hundred thousand board feet daily. And there was a fine new school, an Odd Fellows hall, and a town hall where traveling theatrical troupes frequently staged shows of taste and refinement. There were two railroad depots, five hotels, any number of stores—Hinckley was the main supply point for all the surrounding lumber camps—three churches, and a restaurant any resident would tell you was the equal of anything in Duluth. There were a good number of saloons, too; most of the townspeople probably didn't know how many, say eight or ten.

Despite these advantages—advantages that would have been inconceivable to the rough, enduring men and women who hacked the first clearings out of the forest less than a generation earlier—it was not a particularly happy season for the people of Hinckley.

They were struggling through the driest, hottest summer on record. Autumn with its winds and cool streaked skies was distant, was hidden somewhere beyond the choking clouds of dust that every wagon wheel, every footstep threw up into the still air. There had been no rain to speak of since April; as early as June the mean temperature was the highest the weather bureau down at St. Paul had ever recorded. There was no wind. Cracks opened in the parched streets.

On this, the last day of August, the town woke with dust in its mouth. Husbands and wives had ugly, acrid little squabbles as they got dressed.

Albert Craid, one of Hinckley's two barbers, had just had one. He couldn't remember anymore, as he took off his coat and put on his white jacket, what it was about; he did remember making a poor job of defending his position, whatever it had been. He wiped his hands on his jacket front and looked around the shop. The sun was barely up; dusk still hung in the corners.

The shaving mugs stood in their tall wooden racks between the mirrors, white and gold and shining even in the twilight, each with the name of its owner and a picture of his occupation painted on it. Fire Chief Craig's had a red and yellow hand pumper; John and Charles Peterson, meat dealers, shared a mug on which a steer's head was flanked with a knife and a bone saw; J.W. Stockholm, who ran the Brennan Lumber Company's store, had an intricate exterior view of the store on his—the decorator had done it from a photograph Stockholm had sent; Noble Barrett, the druggist, had a golden mortar and pestle on his; Angus Hay's bore an entire front page of the Hinckley Enterprise, so carefully done that it had cost him five dollars; Tom Dunn, the St. Paul & Duluth telegrapher, had a fine big cup with a sending key on it, improbably surrounded by sprays of lilac.

Craid looked them over, wishing none of their owners any particular joy. He was usually good-natured, but right now his back prickled with heat rash, and he didn't want to cut anybody's hair.

Soon the mill whistle would go, and pull everyone out into the simmering morning.

Beyond town, beyond the depot where the station agent stewed in his sweat and dreamed of being rude to a customer, the lumbermen were already up and working. In the dreary, dun-colored forests, dry pine needles crackled like gravel under their boots. They were all big men, but they felt feeble in the heat. They envied the townspeople spending a nice, soothing day behind their desks and store counters.

Five miles away, where the lumbermen had been working last season, the white pine was gone, and the lesser trees they had felled getting to it lay forgotten in dry heaps. There were miles and miles of this slash—pine needles, branches, bark, all the detritus of lumbering—in the cutover lands around Hinckley. Some of it was burning. Some of it had been burning since May.

Sullen little fires worked their way through the slash, feeding thin smoke into the hazy sky. Every now and again a pile of rubbish would explode into flame, startling a grazing deer. Mostly, though, the fires just wormed along, the way they had every summer since the oldest settler could remember.

Jim Root took the Number Four Limited out of the Duluth station while Jack McGowan, his fireman, tapped at the gauges. The gauges were fine; it was just something he did, every run. He was still new enough to the cab to like to act the part of the railroad man.

"She's lookin' good," said McGowan. Root glanced at the fireman, who stood rubbing his moustache with the back of his glove. The moustache was new; McGowan had started it last winter, and for months it had looked like a streak of grime on his upper lip. Now it had come in full, but Root thought the fireman still looked fifteen. That annoyed him a lot, today.

"Steaming fine," said McGowan.

Root grunted, cracking the throttle a little wider, gathering speed as they rolled through the yards under a hot, gray afternoon sky.

McGowan swung back the firebox door with his shovel, studied the fire, sprinkled in a few lumps of coal. "Goin' nice. Warm work on a day like this, though, you know it?"

Root grunted again.

"What's the matter with you today, Jim? You've been pissy since you got here this A.M."

Ayem? What the hell was that? Was McGowan making up his own railroad slang? "Why don't you just shut up," he said. "I don't want her losing pressure."

"You ever lose pressure with me firing? Jesus. Did you?"

McGowan sulked over to his side of the cab.

Root looked out, saw a string of freight cars pass, and then saw the *Osceola* canted over in a patch of tall brown weeds. Her stack had long since disappeared, and the flanges of her driving wheels were nearly black with rust. But Root could still make out her name in the faint, ruined gleam of gold leaf on her cab. She had been the second, maybe the third, locomotive in the state, and he had driven her years ago. Kept her shiny as a new dime and was as proud of her as a man could be. And now she lay beached, ravaged and abandoned, looking quaint and oddly frail with her dutch-wagon running board. Root shook his head. Her metal wasn't even worth the effort of scrapping her.

He opened the throttle wider, and his right elbow gave him a twinge. It wasn't much—no more than a pinch, really—but it was going to put him out of his cab before too long. He swore to himself. McGowan glanced at him, started to say something, thought the better of it, and reached for his shovel.

A fluke of the sulfurous air pulled coal smoke down around the cab for a moment, making a mirror of the window. Root saw himself: long face, large nose, wide pale forehead. He couldn't see his eyes, just the sockets, black in the black glass.

He'd come on the road at fourteen, back before the Civil War, as an oiler on a Hudson River freight. It had been a scramble in those days, nothing like now with the air brakes and Janney couplers and all. Each time the train stopped he had to squirm under the cars to oil the journals. Sometimes the train would start while he was still underneath, and he would have to grab hold of a brake beam and ride to the next stop with the roadbed streaming along inches beneath him. One time another oiler, a year older than himself, lost his grip up ahead of where Root was hanging on. Root had passed right over his body, cut off at the waist, the eyes still moving.

McGowan fed the fire, hooked the door shut, and slumped into his seat, a man satisfied with tough work well done. Thought that's what stoking meant. He should have been a tallow pot on the Michigan Southern, back when a fireman did a job of work, instead of just sitting around indoors shoveling a little coal now and again. There'd been no lubricators on Michigan Southern locomotives thirty years ago, so when Root wasn't busting his back stoking he was crawling around on the engine, slapping grease on the valves while the locomotive bucked and swayed above the rough roadbed. And there was McGowan, boasting about how he never lost pressure.

Ah, hell, he was being sour. Jack was a good stoker; he did keep his eye on the water.

Still, railroading had gotten pretty soft, by comparison. Single tracks then, and no signals, no telegraph, and no way to tell when you'd be staring into the face of another engine coming at you full tilt. Cornfield meets had been common as derailments in those days. Root remembered having to leap from the cab of a Rogers locomotive—a monster, that was, with six-foot double drivers, cylinders with a thirteen-inch bore, a twenty-two-inch stroke—seconds before it had gone piling into a northbound work train that had dawdled onto the line. He hadn't even had time to look before he leaped into the beautiful May morning, hadn't seen the hillside before it slammed into his back, stunning him for a full minute. He never remembered hearing the sound of the collision, but he'd spent what seemed like an afternoon lying with the breath gone from him, staring upward, seeing the brass bell torn from one of the locomotives way up above him, upside down and absolutely motionless, a golden cup hanging in the blue sky.

"Comin' into Barnum," said McGowan, startling Root.

"Thanks, McGowan. Glad to know the town hasn't changed names since yesterday."

"Well, goddamnit, excuse me, Mr. Engineer Root, but I thought maybe you'd like to whistle or something. You've been on the line for goddamn ever, but it seems to me I'd heard something about whistling when . . ."

Root tugged at the whistle cord before McGowan finished. The fireman was through sulking; he was mad now. And he was right. Root had been woolgathering. He nosed into Barnum and put on the air. The train stopped. The station master took down some baggage while Root watched the loafers sitting on a bench in front of the weathered depot. Waiting for the train was the only thing they did from dawn till dusk, yet they always seemed just bored to death when it arrived.

The town square beyond the depot was scraggly, its grass burned gray-brown by the long, poisonous summer. A stone Union soldier stood brooding there in his cape and forage cap. The Minnesota winters had already worn his hawkish military features into a soft child's face, surprised and open.

"Thirty years gone," said Root.

"What's that?" asked McGowan cheerfully, vindicated as assuaged because Root hadn't barked back at his outburst.

"The war."

"Certainly is a long time back. I was born ten years after the damn thing ended."

It was all history to McGowan. Sherman bulling his way through to the sea was as remote as the Crusades. Root had driven one of Sherman's locomotives, with the general in a coach behind him; he had seen the man with his tight skull's face and inappropriate beard telling his aides to scatter destruction around a brushwood whistle-stop.

Root had pulled the train that took the prisoners from Andersonville to Chattanooga. Gloomiest duty he'd ever had—all those starved men standing terrible-eyed around the train had made him vaguely ashamed that he hadn't gotten hurt himself.

The conductor waved his hand. Root pulled the whistle cord twice, and left the station loafers to whatever they did between trains. He thought of the spring of '65, when the crowded, often incomprehensible war schedules began to let up.

The train never went anywhere. The Union had plenty of trains by then. Fired up and ready to go in the morning, Root's engine would stand on its spur all day, while Root sat talking women or whiskey or different roads with the crew.

"I heard of a place in . . ."

". . . black garters, and nothing else . . ."

". . . the big one, he's getting confused, so he . . ."

". . . green, God, you never saw green like that . . . ."

The engine ticked and hissed behind them, and every so often, at a bored and obligatory nod from Root, the fireman would climb up on the desk and throw in another log. The ash spilled slowly from the stack, drifting down around their feet. Other crews wandered by, offering a plug of tobacco or a whore's long white glove in exchange for some gossip and coffee. Hundreds of ready locomotives tilted imperceptibly toward the wet earth; acres of equipment—tenders, trucks, handcars, boxcars, armored cars—stood idle in the weak, sweet sunlight.

It all made Root terribly restless.

"Coming up on Moose Lake," said McGowan. "They're all the same, except sometimes the depot's on the other side of the track. I swear, Jim, I don't know why you left the East."

"They're all the same in the East, too."

McGowan produced a careful laugh. "I'll bet there's more to it than that. I'll just bet there is." Then, thinking he might have overstepped, he took up the shovel and peered into the firebox as though the slightest darkening of the coals might cost him his life.

Root saw him poised against rage, and smiled. He was probably the best young fireman on the line. His youth wasn't his fault. "Well," Root said, "the war knocked me loose, and I came West to visit an uncle out to Stillwater. Met Emily there, and took a job till I could marry her, and till they built this road."

McGowan stared at him. They'd never talked about anything except schedules, railroad personnel, and maintenance.

"I worked in a sawmill," said Root.

"A sawmill." McGowan started to smile, then stopped. "Not bad work."

"Bad work. Soon as I heard they were building this road, I joined up."

"Good road," said McGowan neutrally, pleased and embarrassed by the intimacy.

Root had started as a dispatcher on the St. Paul & Duluth, and the next year he took an engine out on the road. He'd been an engineer for the St. P. & D. ever since.

Well, he wouldn't be one much longer.

He stared down the clear right-of-way, saw a stand of trees slowly draw close, then volley past. It had all gone like that. He had felt his spell as a mill hand was lasting forever while he did it; but looking back, it had just come up and gone by in a rush, and was lost behind him along with the lurching brake beams of the Hudson River freights and the primitive gauges on Sherman's wood-burners.

He was worn out, that's what the doctor had said.

"This rheumatism isn't getting any better," Root had said to Emily the night before. "It's still stiff in the mornings, and it's starting to hurt some."

"You should see the doctor tomorrow," she told him, alarmed.

"This rumatiz certain sure to be the death of me," he said in the accents of her grandmother, which he knew would make her laugh.

But he did see the doctor the next day. He'd been hoping for some jokes about getting old, but the doctor didn't joke with him. He prodded at the elbow and tapped it with a rubber hammer and eventually made a small, sad humming noise.

"What's the matter?" asked Root.

"Nothing good, I'm afraid." The doctor took off his glasses. "Mr. Root, you're worn out."

"What?" Root thought of steam valves, driving wheel tires and boxes, eccentric straps, truck wheels, wearing away, rusting out, being replaced.

"It's the ulnar nerve at the point of your elbow—"

"My funny bone, you mean?"

"Yes, but it's a nerve, not a bone. And the tissue around it is worn away, so that the nerve is rubbing against the bones of the elbow. It will start to hurt you more before long. I'm sorry, but when it does, you won't be able to do any heavy work. And there isn't a thing in creation any doctor can do about it."

McGowan reached out the window to wave to a six-year-old in a field.

The young men on the road, the young engineers, the ones who had just moved up from fireman, were generally pretty excited about it. They liked to wear flashy bandannas, and salt their conversation with all the railroad slang they knew, and get elaborate whistles with half a dozen pipes so they could quill their own tunes. They liked to think of trainmen hearing a particular whistle and saying, "There's old so-and-so, right on the advertised and going like a bat out of hell." Root had never heard a trainman say anything like that, and he didn't care whether anybody said it about him. He wasn't much for show.

Engine driving was the job he knew best, that was all. The kids who gaped up at him around the water tank—they should join the circus if they wanted excitement. Railroading was reading dispatches, knowing the engine, keeping on time, being responsible to the company for the company's property. A job.

But now, with God knew how few runs left before him, Root realized how much it all meant to him—the talk in the shop under the booming ventilator fans, walking around the engine in the dark with all the light bouncing up off the ground from fires underneath machinery, checking your watch against the conductor's, going out blind through the yard in the fog with the dry chug of the exhaust right there in the cab with you.

When he began to fail, they'd take him off the limited and put him on a switch engine. And then he'd have to throw her over into reverse hundreds of times a day instead of just a few, and the goddamned nerve would go, and that would be that.

He'd join the *Osceola* on the scrap heap.

". . . So the coon pulls out the eel instead, and he looks down at it and says, 'Ah knowed you wuz big, and ah knowed you wuz black, but ah nevah knowed you had little blue eyes befo'.' "

The fat man started to laugh at his own joke. Scott Keegan had heard that laugh for the first time just as the train left Duluth, and already he was sick to death of it. It began with a spluttering hiss—the fat man's patent attempt to restrain it—and then came out big and hearty, "Paugh, paugh, paugh," with the man showing lots of yellow teeth, and spit jiggling in the corners of his mouth. More often than not he would drop his cigar in his lap. This time he almost did, but caught it in his fist while it teetered on his lower lip. It burned his hand when he grabbed it, and he swore. Keegan, who had been straining to produce a grin, laughed out loud.

The fat man (Keegan had caught his name as "Pudgy LaMoo" when he introduced himself, and while he was sure that couldn't be right, he didn't care enough to ask again), spat on the palm of his hand and wiped it on his pants leg. "Little blue eyes," he said, "that's a humdinger. Puts me in mind of another good one . . . ." And off he went into a story about three Negroes daring each other to spend the night in a haunted house. LaMoo rolled his eyes and roared out dialect while Keegan kept his mouth hooked up into a terrible-feeling smirk and tried to avoid catching the eye of the black porter who stood gravely at the end of the chair car. Pine trees jolted slowly past the windows. Keegan cracked his knuckles and squirmed on the plum-colored plush of his seat, which, if it got one degree hotter, was sure to burst into flames around him. "Dat am 'zackly what ah don' wan' do." The ride was lasting as long as Columbus' voyage.

Hiss. Paugh. LaMoo had finished his joke. Keegan laughed, his throat feeling dusty. LaMoo started another.

If I had the sand, thought Keegan, I could simply say to this clown, in a reasonable way, Look, neighbor, one more joke and I'll break your nose. But Keegan was a salesman and his job was making people like him, trust him, think him a hell of a fine fellow. If people didn't like him, he went hungry. Being likable was a hard habit to break.

Keegan was a drummer for the Kraut & Dohnal Barber Supply Company of Chicago. He'd just come from smiling his way through three days of trying to sell Kraut & Dohnal products to barbers in Duluth. They had been bored, occasionally sullen; it had been all he could do to get them to take a catalog or two. He had stood, half delirious with the heat—a great big lake right at the front door, and Duluth was still the hottest place he'd ever been—in a dozen shops, offering bored barbers wild discounts, hints of ripsnorting good times should they ever hit Chicago, every enticement he could think of. And he had come away with a single order for a shaving mug with a painting of a rooster on it. Ninety cents. Seventy-five cents for Kraut & Dohnal, fifteen cents for Keegan.

Hiss. Paugh. LaMoo finished a joke about two newlyweds and an otter. Keegan leered; he found a ribald response to a smutty joke easier to counterfeit than the hearty, honest laughter a coon joke demanded. Had the train stopped? No, it was wheezing along, barely keeping ahead of the next ice age.

"That's a peach," said Keegan, loathing himself and his job.

Twenty years earlier, newly arrived in Averill Park, New York, with his parents, Keegan had found two things he liked about his new home. The boys there hadn't known the first thing about spinning tops, and the drummers came by pretty often. They'd bounce off the train in their mustard-colored suits, smelling of big city restaurants and full of stories. One had seen a young fighter named John L. Sullivan take John Flood on a barge anchored in the Hudson while a police boat bore down on the illegal match; one had come grim from the wreckage at Ashtabula, Ohio, where the *Pacific Express* had run off a bridge in a blizzard; one had dropped a couple of Kiowas in Indian Territory—just part of the job.

Keegan's father—sole owner and proprietor of Keegan's Averill Park Hardware—had asked the Indian fighter drummer if it wasn't tough going.

"Naw, not so tough," the man had said, with the long, glossy scar on his forehead belying his modesty. "Hell, I remember coming on a busted prospector, near dead of thirst. 'Help me?' he croaked.

"You bet I helped him. Told him to start a store. Let him write three thousand worth of orders without putting down a penny. He set up his store, and when I passed by that way a year later, there was pumps and stables and everything, and he was selling corner lots for five apiece. He's still one of my best customers. Started a town name of Omaha."

Keegan's father bought the story—and a lot of hacksaws and a wholly unsalable thing called a caloric engine besides—but Scotty Keegan bought it more. He saw the loafers and the sports dogging the salesman around town, and all he wanted after that was to be a drummer.

No wish ever came true easier.

"So she says, you just wait till Granny's asleep, and I'll show you what I mean—"

LaMoo paused, smirking, and glanced over his shoulder to make sure railroad bulls weren't waiting to arrest him for telling this particular scorcher. Keegan, incapable of another laugh, interrupted the joke.

"Say," he heard himself bellowing, "who'd you sell for?"

"What do I sell for?" LaMoo winked, apparently perfectly happy to abandon the joke. "Well, before I tell you, how's about a cigarette?"

"No, thanks."

"No, c'mon, have one." LaMoo thrust a packet at Keegan.

"I don't want one."

"Friend, I'll tell you, this is no ordinary cigarette. Go on. Take it."

Keegan reached out, took hold of a cork-tipped cigarette, and pulled it. It came out about half an inch, and then, with a thin chime, a small devil sprang out of the packet and bobbled back and forth, red paper thumb glued to its red paper nose.

LaMoo started his hiss. Drained finally of all artificial bonhomie, Keegan leaned back in his seat.

"Now, that's a goddamned silly thing," he said wearily. "Do you really make money on that?"

LaMoo looked mildly hurt. "I work for the Grand Central Novelty Company, out of Lockport, New York," he said. "We have a nifty line of amusements. The Surprise Cigarette Package is only one. We've got others, real knee-slappers, you ought to see the Surprise Inkwell. And we also carry a line of first-rate watches, and a complete line of secret society rings."

He paused. Keegan wanted to say "Sounds nice," but it was just too hot.

LaMoo's broad, jolly face seemed to dwindle. He, too, sank back into the incandescent plush.

"It's all right," he said quietly, "if you know all the jokes. If you're funny, people think they can be funny too, if they buy the stuff."

"I guess I already know a lot of the jokes," said Keegan.

"Aw, hell, sure you do. I just try to keep in practice." He tossed his cigar into the aisle. "People buy pretty good in the fall. Otherwise, it's a pull."

"I sell for Kraut and Dohnal," said Keegan. "Barber supplies. Pretty hard to turn things over in the summer."

LaMoo tugged his collar away from his neck. "It's always tougher than it should be. Not that I'd do anything else. I like the traveling."

"What do you like about it?"

La Moo smiled the first real smile Keegan had seen since they left Duluth. It showed a lot less teeth. "I like knowing I don't have to stay long in the towns I go to."

Keegan laughed his first real laugh of the ride. "If the food was better—if it was better anywhere, it might not be so bad. You know what I picked up in Duluth? Fifteen cents in commissions."

"You don't know the business," LaMoo said solemnly. "Me, I know the business. Ran out a good line of talk, saw everybody. I came out of Duluth with thirty-three cents in my pocket."

"You heading for Hinckley?"

"Sure. Bound to pick up a dollar there. Put it together with the Duluth money, buy an estate in the country. Be an inspiration to youth."

"Last year," said Keegan, "I wrote down 'Mass.' and they misread it in Cinci and shipped my sample case to Mississippi. I got to spend a week and a half in a town without a name, waiting for it to come back."

"That's what happened to me. I don't mind it half as much as the roll."

"The roll?"

"The roll they give you for dinner, wherever you eat. It's always like a rock, and I always take a bite, then let it alone. Then, the next hotel I stop at, there it is, waiting for me. So I take another bite, and leave it alone, and there it is again down the line. I swear they have some special train to carry that roll around ahead of me."

"I'll be grateful for that roll, if the season doesn't pick up," said Keegan. "I'm breaking in new territory. The last Kraut man to cover Hinckley was drunk all the time, didn't get off the train there for ten years. You know anything about Hinckley?"

LaMoo pulled out a cigar, scowled at it, and stuck it back in his pocket. "Not the first thing. I know it's the biggest town between Duluth and St. Paul. Twelve, fifteen hundred people. Lumber town."

"When I was a kid," said Keegan, "the drummers always seemed to be happy as clams. People waved good-bye when they got back on the train."

"Aah, I'll bet it wasn't any better then. They still had to leave their families—"

And to Keegan's astonishment, the prince of the dirty joke launched into a lament about having to be away from his family for nine months out of the year. His wife—not pretty the way, say, Jeanie Carron on the Tilton Circuit was pretty, but pretty enough—waiting for him, she and the kids living for his letters.

"I was in the way of being into a good little business in Oneonta. Nice little store. But I didn't want it. No flies on me. Christ, there's kinds of stupid that come back and bite you all your life. Say, do you have a missus?"

"Did," said Keegan.

"Aw," said LaMoo, thinner and calmer than he'd been since Keegan had met him. "Now, I'm sorry. I'm truly sorry."

LaMoo seemed to think she was dead. Well, let him. Keegan said, "I'm not sure I got your name."

"LeMoyne, Jack LaMoyne. But I call myself Pudgy. People won't buy a novelty from a fat man named Jack."

Keegan smiled at the puffy man in the cheap striped suit, both of them glad the jokes had stopped.

Soon the two drummers fell asleep. Just north of Sandstone, Keegan woke with a start, sweaty and disoriented as he always was when he dozed off in the daytime. Great trees scudded past the window, then jerked away as a clearing spun into view.

At its edge, smoke rose in a torpid spiral. Keegan wondered what hardy Minnesota homesteader had the industry to keep a fire going on a day like this. Nobody could be putting up preserves in this weather, he decided, and reached over to nudge LeMoyne.

"Hey," he said, prying his companion from his fat man's dreams of nougats and big leather chairs and cold brown bottles of beer. LeMoyne wiped his loose, flushed face and squinted out the window.

"Christ," he said. "I wish to hell they'd give me the Philadelphia-Boston circuit. Every summer I have to come through here, and every summer there's something burning."

"The trainmen are bound to have seen it," said Keegan. "Won't they send a crew to put it out?"

LeMoyne fished in his coat for a cigar. "Naw. The locals don't seem to give a good goddamn. They'll wait for the snow to do the job."

"But there's forest all around here."

"There's forest all the way to the North Pole. They just don't care." He scowled, then brightened. "Maybe if they're stupid enough not to mind if their homes burn down over their heads, they're stupid enough to spread a lot of coin around for novelties. I've always done pretty well in Hinckley. But I do wish they'd let me go East."

As the train bored back into the forest, sparks from the stack drifted down into the clearing. Most were dead before they touched the ground. A few started small fires in the slash. All but one burned out in minutes. That one began to move sluggishly toward the rising smoke Keegan had seen, which came from the trunk of a fallen jack pine. It had been set afire by embers borne for miles on imperceptible air currents from the place where a farmer was clearing his acreage by burning it over.

The new fire worked toward the jack pine in a wide curve; the flames joined and spread slowly into the woods. The forest floor smoldered, occasionally arcing out low jets of sparks. More smoke rose into the dead air.

Tom Dunn, idling at his key in the bay of the Hinckley depot, listened as the Sandstone operator cleared the Number Four Duluth Limited. "Root's always on the advertised," Dunn said aloud to his desk, unconsciously taking part in the empty, affable telegraphic chatter. The Sandstone and Pokegama operators were talking to each other across him, exchanging banter in Morse. ". . . AND BREAK YOUR NOSE," said Sandstone.

"IF U HAVE A BIG BROTHER AND KNOW WHO HE IS BEST BRING HIM," Pokegama rattled back.

Pokegama lay a few miles down the line, Sandstone a few miles up. Both operators had years on Dunn, and he interrupted their ritual insults only during quiet times, and then only when he had his message clear in his head and could tap it out quickly. Dunn was a good enough brass pounder, but he knew he couldn't talk through the key with the careless ease of those old home guards.

For one thing, he'd had barely half an apprenticeship. His father was a butcher, and would have liked Tom to be a butcher too. As a boy, Tom had loved hanging around the shop, watching his father skin off the fat from a joint with a worn, pale scary little knife. He'd liked watching his father slap the meat on glossy white paper and pull the twine out of the red mouth of the tin black man that hung from the ceiling. Liked the jokes his father made with the customers:

"Warm weather please you, Mr. Dunn?"

"More than a sharp stick in the eye, ma'am."

But even playing around in the sawdust on the floor and going in to watch his breath in the cold locker where the carcasses hung white and purple, Tom knew he didn't want to be a butcher. He would have liked to be one if he was one, but he didn't want to learn how. If he could suddenly have become his father, just like that, suddenly have been the portly, able man who tossed the counterweights on the scale and made good small talk, it would have been fine. But he understood early that before you could become such a figure you had to spend your days hauling half a cow around on your back behind the shop, while your father shouted at you all the time.

So Tom helped sweep out the store when he had to, but he spent the rest of his time down at the station with the other boys. *There* was a job. The pompous, negligent swank of the locomotive nosing in, spilling steam and hot dirt; the brass checks glinting as the station-master pulled them off the luggage, the engineer in his cab thumbing contemptuously through his orders.

Once, when Tom was nine, the engineer had dropped his orders and the wind carried them underneath the locomotive. Tom crawled in after them, under sizzling pipes and caked grease, found them being buffeted against the forward driving wheel by a jet of stream. He grabbed them, scrambled back terrified into the daylight, and handed the sopping papers to the conductor. The conductor passed them up to the engineer, who studied them, scratched the back of his neck, and then looked gravely down on Tom.

"These are pretty important orders, boy," he said. "Always good to have dealings with a real railroad man who knows about orders. Now come on and thank him, Billy." The fireman leaned out to wave his gratitude to Tom while the engineer whistled twice and started up. If Tom had ever had any future as a butcher, it died right there.

The boy hung around the station night and day after that, and except for old Schwertfeger, he was the only one around when Sy Hornby blew into town. Schwertfeger took the night trick at the depot. He'd been there since the line went through in '69, and he had started out as the day operator—the only operator, since the depot shut down at eight in those days.

Now he drowsed away the night over the quiet key, stirring only when his cough started, jolting him closer to the grave each time it took him. Tom hated the thin, violent noise and would have left that night, except the southbound freight was due through any minute.

The cough wouldn't quit, so Tom went out to wait on the platform.

Hornby didn't come on the train. He just came walking down the tracks. Tom was playing mumbledepeg with the only knife he had ever owned. He'd traded Orrie Guyer for it, a fine agate marble and he regretted the trade. The knife had a broken point; every time he pitched it the useless thing danced on the gray boards of the platform for a second, and then fell over on its side.

"That's one punk knife," a voice said. "I'd be scared to go up against an angry carrot with a knife like that."

Tom squeaked and turned to see a tall ragged man standing a little ways off from him, grinning. The man was dressed in awful clothes, but otherwise he looked like anybody else, except that the hair on the left side of his head was an unremarkable dingy brown, and the hair on the right was bright silver-white.

"Evenin'," Tom mumbled, remembering to be polite.

"Evenin' to you," the man said. "This Hinckley?"

"Yes, sir."

"What are you doing up and about?"

That was plain impertinent from a stranger, and Tom knew it. "Nothing," he said. And then, brave because his father was the butcher, he added, "What are *you* doing?"

The gray and brown man laughed. "I'm a brass pounder." He cocked a thumb past his shoulder at Schwertfeger, dozing in his bay. "And I bet I'm one hell of a lot better than that old loon."

Tom, appalled, said, "Why, that's Mr. Schwertfeger."

"Oh now, I'm sorry," the man said solemnly. "What's your name, boy?" Tom told him. "Well I'm sorry, Tom Dunn, because I didn't know that was Mr. Schwertfeger, and I surely meant no offense. But I bet I have the edge on him in the telegraphy department."

He knelt down and rattled his knuckles against the platform. "Know what that was?"

"No," said Tom.

"That was, 'Good to meet you, Mr. Dunn.'"

"Morse?" Tom asked, awed.

"Didn't get it?"

Tom shook his head.

"Sa'll right—I'll bet Mr. Sweatfinger wouldn't have got it, either."

"Schwertfeger," said Tom. "Just teach me the 'good,' that's all, then I'll go away, please."

"You want to be a lightning slinger, Tom?"

Most grown-ups called him Tommy, even though he always introduced himself as Tom.

"No, sir," he said. "I want to be an engineer."

The man snorted. "Course you would."

Tom wondered what had annoyed him.

"Listen, you sit up in the engine, you're not driving it like you would a buggy. You can't turn anywhere. You just look out the window and go along. If it wasn't for us brass pounders, half the engineers in the world would be dead right now."

Tom nodded.

"Know why?"

Tom shook his head.

"Because it's the people at the key keep the roads open, tell the engineers when to go and when to stop. All along the line, lightning slingers are keeping track of the trains, making sure the road's clear, making sure nothing goes wrong." He pointed off down the track toward Pokegama. "There's not a hogger running that line can go a yard if the brass pounder don't give him his orders. Now, you want to learn how to do 'good'?"

"Sure," said Tom. After all, the engineer had said the orders he fetched from under the locomotive were important.

"Good." The man closed his big had around Tom's little one and started knocking the boy's knuckles gently against the platform. "That's the G—don't worry about going too fast at first—and that's the O—simple, the O—and there it is again, and that's the *D*. Now do it yourself."

Tom got the G and the *D*, but forgot the O.

"That's just fine," said the man. "I can tell already you've got the head for it. Now, O—"

"What's your name?" asked Tom.

" 'Scuse me, Tom. It's Hornby. Sy Hornby. Now, start with the G, if you still remember it . . ."

Tom went home that night exalted and couldn't get to sleep: he kept tapping GOOD GOOD GOOD on his bedpost.

Hornby loafed around town buying drinks for people until his money ran out. Then he worked at Gifford's livery stable, and lived above it, until old Schwertfeger got sick. Then he became the Hinckley operator and began to educate Tom.

"Write 'When in the course,'" he said once.

"That's not an order," said Tom, eleven now and cheeky.

"Did I say it was?" Hornby had an empty bottle on the desk in front of him, had for three weeks. He pointed at it. "Going to build a ship in that. It's easy, when you know how."

"It's not easy," Tom said. "The masts all have to stand up."

"You put 'em in flat, with little tiny threads tied to 'em. Then you just pull, and up they come. You want sails, you put them on first, too."

Hornby handed him a pencil and a blotter. "Write this," he said. He drummed his knuckles on the table. Tom got down "Hold 17 at" before Hornby snatched the blotter away from him and read it. "That's too slow," he said. "By the time you get that finished and out, everybody's dead. Now look, you have to write like this."

He wrote slowly, each word joined together by loops that dipped down beneath the line. "It looks too fancy," he said, "but it's the only way to write fast and have it clear enough for the trainmen to read. You can read that, the way I've written it?"

Tom nodded.

"Now I'll do it fast." Hornby threw his hand across the blotter like a gesture and left behind on the gray paper, clear and connected, "Hold 17 at Sandstone for orders."

Tom whistled.

Tom practiced when he could. He brought his efforts, scrawled on heavy brown paper, to Hornby, and Hornby always said they looked fine, checked him for speed, and told Tom he had to do it quicker.

In the fall of '89, when Tom was sixteen, the St. P. & D. put a day man on at Hinckley, a company slug who was all Adam's apple and thick glasses and cheap, fussy clothes. Sy Hornby was moved up to the night shift, and that made Tom sore.

"You've earned yourself the day trick," he said to Hornby, who just looked amused about it. "Why are you stuck here all night?"

Hornby nodded toward the empty bottle. "President Cleveland sent me a letter on behalf of the company. He said they couldn't trust a day man who promised to build a ship in a bottle and then didn't. Happens every day. Now take the key, and O.S. old Root. Watch how you do it, too. He appreciates quality."

Tom had begun to take the key more and more while Hornby read or dozed or puttered around the office. "You're a fair operator now," Hornby said, "but I suspect you'll always be a little slow."

Tom complained about that, but Hornby assured him that he was still better than many on the line. Even so, it didn't sit well with Tom.

Slow or not, he took over the night trick the next summer. If asked, he would have said he'd welcome any turn of chance that made him a railroad man. But the way he got his job saddened him every time he thought of it.

It was a stifling August evening, and a storm had been building all day, announcing its coming with weak stirrings of thunder miles away toward Lake Superior. Even the light work of sweeping the store brought the sweat out on Tom. The cat lay on the counter trapped in his fur, his side heaving. As Tom went to lock up, he stopped to poke a finger in the animal's stomach. "Mice'll have free run tonight, hey, Simon?" Simon made a hot little burp of protest.

Tom stepped out front, locked the door, and glanced at the round, heavy clouds that were piling up on each other, with thin blue lights running between them. "Come on," he said, rubbing his damp neck. "Get it over with."

He put the key in his pocket, looked through the dark window at the stunned cat, and started off up the street to the depot.

As he went up the steps a fat raindrop smacked him on the cheek.

He stepped inside. Sy looked up from the key.

"Not a minute too soon, I'd say. How're . . ."

Whatever Sy was asking disappeared in a torrent of noise and water. Thunder slammed overhead, shaking the building. The roof started to leak right away. Sy tilted his head toward the sounder.

"What're they saying?" asked Tom.

"It's Sandstone. Wants us to know it's raining."

Water poured down the windows of the depot bay. "Bad night for the brakemen," Tom said.

"Bad night for everybody. Be glad you're indoors. Imagine old Root out on the road. He's quacking like a duck right now, but there's not a thing he can do about it. It's cooler already. And we're indoors. This"—Sy pointed to the key—"this here is the best job a railroad man can have. Sorry you're not a fireman tonight, Tom?"

Tom shook his head. Thunder came crashing down the sky and made his ears ring.

The door swung open. A short, wet woman in an elaborate hat stood before them. She had big breasts and a round face and was somewhere in her thirties. Tom thought she might have been very pretty once, and then decided that she was probably pretty now, since he had never before in his life thought about what a woman might have looked like when she was younger.

"That you, Sy?" she asked.

Sy looked at her; his mouth dropped open.

"Naw," he managed, "it's another Sy Hornby with half a head of gray hair."

"I knocked, but nobody answered," she said.

"There's a storm," said Tom quickly, not wanting to hear Sy say anything else in that voice and with that look on his face. She didn't even glance Tom's way.

"How are you, Sy?"

"Pretty fair. What're you doing here, Lisa?" He stood up. The sounder started to rattle. "Take that, will you, Tom? I'm going out for a while."

"Take it? Myself?"

Sy gave him a terrible grin. "Hell, yes, sure." He backed Lisa out the door and shut it behind them. Tom sat at the desk.

Everybody was calling in, all up and down the line. The rain wasn't helping, but everything was going wrong anyway. Somebody had pulled a drawbar below Pine City. The limited was late, so some hotshot had taken a three-car freight out of the hole onto the main line without clearance, which would hang up the limited somewhere, and the brass would be mad as hell. Later, the drawbar got fixed, but by then a lot of hoggers were hot to make up time and everything came at Tom fast and foggy.

He handled the key the best he could, biting at his lip until it bled, while the thunder battered away and the lightning gave him brief, hellish glimpses of the tracks in front of him. With each flash he expected to see some lurid tragedy of his own making. He came close to weeping with relief when Hornby returned around eleven.

He didn't feel relieved long, though, because Hornby was drunk. Not yelling and singing drunk, but a bit slow and too cheerful.

"Bad night, Tom?"

"Pretty bad."

"Well, you appear to have done a yeoman's job. Not exactly sure what a yeoman is, but I know he wouldn't make much of an operator. Bows and arrows, isn't that what yeomen do? Gimme the chair."

Tom got up slowly. Sy bumped his knee against the desk as he sat down, cursed, giggled, and asked Tom what was going on.

"Pokegama says—"

"Shut up. Never mind. I'll dope it out."

Sy grabbed the key and worked it too fast for Tom to follow. The sounder crackled into life. Sy laughed. "Horrible piss-end of a mess. Don't worry, Sy Hornby's the Hinckley operator, and everything will be right as rain soon." He pointed out the bay at the rain and laughed. "Not bad, huh?"

Afterward, Tom always thought that if he'd been a quicker operator, he could have figured out what was happening, have gotten the key back from Sy, and fixed things. He was just about to ask Sy what was wrong when the big consolidation came shouldering in, its cab boiling with rain. Steam fumed up around the head lamp and made the beam of light look dusty.

"Stinking night for those boys," said Sy. He tapped the key, listened to the answer, scribbled something on a flimsy, and handed it to Tom. "Take that out, would you, Tommy?"

Tom almost refused, just because of the "Tommy," but then, not wanting a squabble with Sy, he took the order. He was thoroughly drenched by the time he got to the cab. He reached up and the engineer reached down, took the paper from him, and scowled at it. The man looked to be about nineteen, and Tom was jealous. Tom waved, the engineer raised his glove, ducked back into the cab, and opened the throttle. When Tom entered the depot, knuckling rainwater from his eyes, the sounder was going and Sy was grinning at it. "Never heard such a ruckus in all my life." He tapped the key. "There'll be some lost revenue tonight. Makes you heartsick, thinking of all those good investors, perhaps losing twenty, thirty cents apiece. Well, they can always take it out on their maids and such. Nothing makes—"

The sounder started. Tom, listening to Sy, didn't catch the message. Sy looked at Tom, a smile still hanging on his face.

"Goddamn," he said softly through the smile. "Sweet Jesus, I've done it."

"Done what?"

Sy turned back to the key and worked it furiously. Through the clockwork, spinning noise, Tom picked up the words "doctors," "ready," and—after Sy had hoisted his watch out of his vest and glanced at it—"seven minutes."

The sounder started as soon as Sy stopped, but Sy paid it no attention. He got to his feet.

"It's yours," he said.

"What?"

"The key. The job. Look." He pointed to the bottle in which he was always about to build the ship. "That's the last whiskey I ever had, till tonight. Look out for whiskey."

He turned to the desk, picked up a pencil, and scribbled on a piece of paper in his operator's script: "I was at the key and have sole responsibility for the wreck. Seymour Hornby."

"What wreck?" Tom asked, and then: "Seymour?"

"Oh," said Sy. He turned to the paper, scratched out the

"Seymour," and replaced it with an S.

"What wreck?" Tom asked again.

"I put the freight on the track with the limited. Pokegama cleated the limited. They'll meet head on."

Tom jumped for the key.

"Can't help. You know that. There's no station between 'em now."

Sy put on a ratty flannel hat. "Good luck, Tom. You'll be busy tonight. It's a real job—it's no ribbon clerk's job. I've killed a bunch of people tonight."

The sounder was going again, and Tom was already in the chair. He didn't see Sy Hornby leave.

The whistle sounded up ahead. "Hinckley," called the porter. Keegan grabbed his sample case and the heavy model of the barber chair in its showy mahogany box. LeMoyne lifted down his luggage.

"A million laughs in one small suitcase," he said joylessly. They moved into the aisle as the train pulled up to the station with a series of diminishing jolts.

"Jesus God, but it's hot," said LeMoyne, stepping down onto the depot platform. "It's hotter than it was in the cars."

Keegan wiped his neck with a handkerchief. "They say the earth's getting closer to the sun."

"Well, it's gotten a hell of a lot closer since we left Duluth. The air here"—LeMoyne waved his hand in front of his face—"you can see it, taste it. I want a beer, and I want to drink it in another town."

Keegan drew in a breath. LeMoyne was right about the air; it was dense and gritty. A team coming up the street fifty yards away wavered in a faint haze. Somewhere beyond the town a band saw sang its rising note, thin and shrill in the distance.

"That looks like the hotel," said Keegan, pointing across the street to a large frame building. "Might as well go register."

The locomotive whistled twice, and the train moved out of the station. LeMoyne stood watching it as though it were carrying away his last chance for earthly happiness.

Just outside of town, Root saw a dozen section men shoveling dirt onto the tracks. He slowed as they stepped clear.

"What's going on?" he asked. "Hey there, Bull."

Bull Henly had been the Hinckley section boss for years. He had gotten the job simply because of his size. He was the biggest man Root had ever seen. If he had a temper, nobody Root knew about had ever had the nerve to push him to a point where he might have shown it. Root had once seen him win a pie-eating contest and, twenty minutes later, consume an entire roast chicken.

"Hey, Jim," he said. "Putting out fires along the right-of-way. There's a thousand little fires."

"Happens every summer," said Root.

"Not like this one. There was ties burning up the line. Say, you hoggers have it soft, sitting up there in the breeze, taking it easy."

"That's right, Bull. Nice and cool up here."

Henly waved, and Root started up. After a while, he said to McGowan, "You know, there was nothing doing at the Hinckley depot. I wonder where all the loafers were." McGowan shrugged.

The loafers were at the other depot waiting for the southbound freight. The tracks of the Eastern Minnesota crossed those of the St. Paul & Duluth just south of Hinckley and the town had grown, wedge-shaped, between them. The Eastern Minnesota had a good deal to do with Hinckley's prosperity, but most of the townspeople felt vengeful toward the line.

"It's just the damnedest inconsideration," said Chief John Craig. "We pay their steep rates and they use the money to build a swamp right in the middle of town."

"Well, now, John, it's not right in the middle of town," Noble Barrett said reasonably. "Anyway, the Eastern's bringing you a nice new toy, isn't it?"

Craig nodded. "And bringing it late, just like you'd expect." A tough, weathered man in his mid-fifties, Craig ran the town's fire department. He wore a beard to cover a bizarre wound he had got at Gettysburg thirty years earlier. A bullet had driven through his cheek and out his open mouth, leaving his teeth and jaw undamaged. Somehow the wound had never closed and, when he was feeling testy,

Craig would squirt a stream of tobacco out through the side of his face. He did it now.

"You know," Barrett said mildly, "I don't really see how you can complain about the Eastern making an eyesore when that little performance of yours could make a dog puke."

The eyesore was a three-acre gravel pit the railroad had dug for roadbed material. Despite a score of indignant letters and occasional threats of legal action, the Eastern had never filled it in, and the townspeople were damned if they would. The digging had tapped a sluggish spring and the pit held about an acre of stagnant water.

"Who's doing the poisoning while you're frittering away the day down here, Noble?" Barrett ran a drugstore which, in a poetic spasm, he had named the Star of the Wilderness Pharmacy.

"The boy's minding the store. He'd be happy to make you a stopper for your cheek, gratis—the goodwill'd do wonders for business."

"Too bad about you, Noble. In my business you don't need goodwill." Craig tried to spit again, but found his juice exhausted.

Angus Hay, publisher and editor of the Hinckley *Enterprise*, saw a tremor in the rails and called out, "Here she comes," just before the small crowd heard the whistle.

Number Ninety-four, Will Voge at the throttle, came through the pines. As the train drew up to the station, Voge shouted, "Got something here for you. Don't know how a squatty little town like Hinckley could afford it."

Craig waved. "You got it here so late I bet it don't work anymore."

"Don't matter," yelled Voge, "ain't nothing in this burg worth saving."

Nobody heard him. They were all running down toward the flatcar, where George Turgeon, the Eastern's puffy, complacent depot agent, astonished everyone by leaping up on the car even before the train had stopped and tugging at the ropes dogging down the canvas.

"Attaboy, George," shouted Craig. "Put your back into it."

Two trainmen scrambled down from the adjoining boxcar, and one of them politely edged Turgeon out of the way while the other went to work on the far side. With a nice sense of drama, both pulled the canvas away at the same time, and there was the new fire engine, all polished nickel and fresh paint, glittering like a full brass band.

"Hurrah," said Angus Hay; everyone cheered.

"See how she sparkles," said Craig and, embarrassed, smirked and looked around to see who had heard him.

Barrett had heard and thought of saying that the engine struck him as kind of small. But he liked Craig, and the fire chief seemed close to dancing, and it wasn't such a bad-looking machine after all.

A single-pump engine built by the Waterous Works of St. Paul, it stood on tall red wheels whose spokes were elegantly picked out in gold. Even under the murky sky the steam dome blazed like a meteor, and the needles in the cluster of gauges on the boiler lay canted to the left all at the same neat angle. Resting on the flatcar, the engine looked like one of the great works of man, larger and more powerful than the locomotive that had brought it to Hinckley. The trainmen who had uncovered it stood grinning as though they had built it with their bare hands.

"Looks kind of small," said Barrett, despite himself.

"Sure it does," said Craig, smiling, never taking his eyes off it.

The engine had caused no end of controversy in the town meetings, with Craig stumping for a first-size double that would have required four horses, and the city fathers wondering if they really needed anything more than a hand pumper. Craig, brooding, had finally retreated enough to accept a fourth size that could throw 300 gallons of water per minute. Only his wife, Molly, knew how happy he was not to have had to settle for a fifth size with a 250-gallon capacity.

"A signal day," said Hay, then bent his head to write in his notebook. He started when a wide, fleshy hand dropped on his shoulder and the hand's owner shouted out, "Signal, indeed!"

LeMoyne, who could read a selling situation quickly, stepped around in front of Hay and spoke to Craig. "A signal day, and a splendid machine. I'm just out of Chicago—some big town, boys. They just got an engine there that could eat this one and never—"

"Whynch'ya go back to Chicago, then, mister?"

"Because I loathe Chicago, friend. Let me finish. That big engine came into Chicago and not a soul in the city turned out to greet it.

Four, five men unloaded it like it was just another sack of offal." LeMoyne looked indignant, then turned to give Hinckley's new pumper two seconds of reverent study. "Here we have a smaller engine coming in, and the whole town is here to see it. All I'm saying is—it's this kind of spirit keeps a pinewood city standing when a brick and mortar one can burn to the ground."

He got a cheer, ignored it, and spoke to Craig. "Sorry. I guess I got carried away. I know I have no business butting in here, but it makes a man happy, sometimes, to see something like this."

"Don't believe we've met," said Craig, cautious but not about to offer offense to this eloquent, straight-thinking stranger.

"Name's LeMoyne. They call me Pudgy, but I can't guess why." LeMoyne heard some laughter. "I'm just a drummer, handle a nice little line of novelties. Jokes mostly."

"My name's Craig. I'm chief of the fire department here."

They shook hands. "Well, I guess the department's just about twice as good as it was an hour ago."

"Wouldn't go that far," said Craig. "We have a good old hand pumper. Always did right by us."

"Bet it did," LeMoyne said quickly, "with Minnesota muscle behind it. But it just can't match steam. Nothing can."

Craig nodded. "That's right."

LeMoyne had been nearly shouting, but even so people were starting to move away to watch the trainmen unload the engine. He took the plunge, raising his voice enough to make Craig move back a step.

"Like I said, I sell jokes, but I have a real special watch with a dandy steam pumper on the back. Watch has sixteen jewels, and the pumper is put on perfect—not punched out, but brass laid on the nickel. Comes pretty steep, this watch, so I don't carry one around with me. But look at this picture."

He thrust a catalog at Craig and stuck a finger at the cut that showed "the Fireman's Ordinary Watch." He held the finger over the word "ordinary."

"I've got a good watch," said Craig.

"And you had a good fire engine. You've got a new one now, and I'm thinking the watch might suit the day. Any engraving's free.

Might want to put the date and the name of the company on it."

"How much?"

"Well, that's the trouble. It's steep." LeMoyne frowned and scratched his head. He took his time figuring, knowing that once someone asked a price, he wouldn't leave until he'd gotten it.

"They go for twelve dollars in St. Paul," he said finally, "and they're worth it. But I travel a lot, and a traveling man'll tell you it's nice to sleep in a town you feel safe in. And if some of the men in your company wanted one too, I guess I could get them to you for seven and a half. At that price, it's a ten-cent commission for me. The smart boys in the office'll say I'm an awful fool. But what's the fun in life if you can't be a fool once in a while?"

Craig looked at him. LeMoyne slumped some and wiped his forehead with his sleeve, an embarrassed man who'd gotten carried away and talked a little too much.

"Hey," Craig said, "Mike, Noble, come over here. I'd like you to look at something."

Tom Turgeon, the ill-natured brother of the Eastern depot agent, ran Hinckley's classiest barbershop. It made him sore as hell that Albert Craid's mangy shop did the better business. Not on the weekends, of course, when every barber in town had all the customers he could handle; but this Friday afternoon Turgeon knew that anyone free to get a haircut was getting it from Craid. An able and tireless worker, Turgeon was constitutionally incapable of understanding how people could forsake his spotless parlor for Craid's fogged mirrors and gummy combs. The fact that Craid was, according to Turgeon's strict lights, a grinning buffoon should have had no bearing on the matter, and Turgeon never considered it. He had set up a shop the equal of anything in St. Paul. He had staffed it with cowed and attentive barbers—three of them. He presided over the fourth chair nearest the window, but every chair had its own hand-painted Bohemian glass shaving-paper vase, and each barber wielded a full-concaved razor made of Bohler Austrian steel. All this was more than any reasonable customer should expect, and if the men of Hinckley didn't come around, sooner or later Turgeon could pull up stakes and open a shop in Duluth that would be a magnet to that town's gentlemen.

Scott Keegan could scarcely have picked a worse customer for the approach he had in mind.

Hot, weary, a heavy case in each hand, Keegan glanced in the window, saw four empty chairs, and stepped inside.

"Yes, sir. Good afternoon." A man stepped forward. He was wearing a white jacket which, Keegan noticed, was every bit the equal of Kraut & Dohnal's Military Coat Number 200, top of the line at $1.75 each.

"Afternoon," said Keegan. "I'd like a shave." He sat in the chair nearest the window. The barber took hold of the bar and tilted him back. Keegan screamed.

The barber jumped away. "What's wrong?"

"Let me up! Let me up!"

"Jesus, mister, what's the matter?" The barber threw the handle back and Keegan climbed out of the chair. He stood bent over, rubbing his back and moaning. "Damn, I could have been killed. Who owns this shop?"

"I do, mister," said his barber. "Name's Turgeon, like it says outside. Now, just what in the hell is the matter?"

"What's the matter? What's the matter?" Keegan straightened up grimacing. "It's a miracle you didn't break my back with that machine. How old is that chair?"

"Less than a year." That wasn't good, but Keegan persisted.

"Well, no wonder your shop's empty. No wonder you've had complaints."

Turgeon, scowling, said, "Yours is the first. Now just what's your business?"

"My business right now is to save you from a peach of a lawsuit. I represent the Kraut and Dohnal Barber Supply Company of Chicago—"

"Ah!" Turgeon's scowl deepened, turning his whole face into vertical wrinkles. "So you're a goddamned drummer and you have the crust to—"

"Just a minute. Just a minute." Keegan grabbed for the mahogany case that held the model barber chair. "This'll interest you." He flipped open the catches, threw back the lid, and lifted out a perfect replica of the Congress Pedestal Hydraulic Chair. All the tiny, beautifully turned fittings flashed as he set it on the marble shelf of the wall case. He pumped the lever and the seat rose with tiny majesty. "Hydraulic," he said proudly.

Generally the Congress Chair was a great crowd pleaser. One of the other barbers whistled, but Turgeon was unmoved. "That so a cat can get haircut?" he asked.

Keegan, startled, said, "No, no, it's a model," then, feeling stupid, went into his harangue. "This is one of our most popular patterns. It's sturdy, handsome, and virtually indestructible. Look at those flatboard and footrest plates—solid cast brass. That's what we mean by quality at Kraut and Dohnal. It's quartersawn white oak—"

"Hah," said Turgeon. "Quartersawn white oak. What about a porcelain base? Where's the one with the porcelain base?"

"Kraut and Dohnal prefers the warmth and sturdiness of wood to—"

"Kraut and Dohnal hasn't got around to selling porcelain-base chairs yet because it's a small, poky company. But Koken has, and I bought 'em from Koken. Look there. Look at the killer chair—brand-new and all porcelain. Now get the hell out of my shop."

Keegan looked at the chairs with their shiny white bases. The office had been telling him for two years that Kraut & Dohnal would be selling them soon. St. Paul was one thing, but who would have expected them to turn up in a lumber town?

"Well, come to that, they're fine-looking chairs. Hope you didn't take my little joke amiss. Now, you'll be needing soap, strops, mugs."

"When I need 'em, I'll get 'em from Koken."

Never Say Die Keegan. He wished he could stop himself, but the habits went too deep. "Well, I'll just leave our catalog with you. It's a new one, and there are some first-rate new things in it." He opened his sample case, set a catalog on the shelf, picked up the chair, put in its box, and made for the door. "We have some new clippers in there that are the envy of the industry. Keep it, look at it, enjoy it. Mighty fine to have met you, Mr. Turgeon."

As he stepped out the door the catalog flapped past his ear and landed in the street at his feet. Feeling his neck burning, he picked it up, dusted it off, and put it back in the sample case. He glanced at the store across the street. "'Star of the Wilderness Pharmacy,'" he said aloud. "Shit. Hinckley, shit."

Gus Lindstrom had come to Hinckley in 1875 and for a while had made a pretty good go of farming south of the town. But when his wife died trying to bear him a child—it would have been a son—he lost his stomach for farming. He went down to Minneapolis, where he found a job in flour mills harsh enough to send him back every night to his boardinghouse with no thoughts at all in his head.

He left behind a small barn and a small house, made of lumber cheap even by the standards of an area where all lumber was cheap.

Nels Hjerpa, out for an angry prowl after one of the many marital squabbles in Hinckley that morning, was surprised to come upon both house and barn burned to black ovals in the earth. The fire hadn't been too recent; the scorched ground was no warmer than the grass around it. Hjerpa scuffed through the ash where the house had been, remembering how proud poor old Gus had been of the curtains his wife had brought from Sweden.

Then he went to where the barn had stood. Gus had sold most of his tools before he left, but Hjerpa found a metal thing in the cinders. He turned it over and over in his hands, and finally decided it once had been the blade of a hoe.

He wondered about the kind of fire that could melt a hoe.

It didn't seem to have come from anywhere in particular. All around, the woods stood dry but whole.

Hjerpa smelled smoke. He shook his head, dropped the hoe, and walked off over Lindstrom's old rutabaga patch, ready to make things up with Karin.

Jemmy Stockholm trudged home from the berry patch through the dun acreage of summer, bored and jaded from the long season. It was hot; it had always been hot; it would always be hot; and he was sick to death of dry, rasping grass and the curdled green scum along the banks of Grindstone Creek. He would turn eleven years old on the seventeenth of October, but that was the only fun he could foresee, and it seemed as remote to him as the advent of the regularly scheduled transatlantic balloon flights he had read about in *Scientific American.* Snow, Christmas, sledding, and the wonderful ruby patterns the Art Garland stove threw on the parlor carpet were too painfully distant even to bear thinking on.

He remembered thinking, back around the Fourth of July, about how he wished the summer could last forever. Now it was, and he felt betrayed by his wish. It made him grave, thinking about what you wanted and then about how you felt when you got it.

There was an interesting speckled rock lying in the middle of the patch in front of him. Momentarily cheered, he picked it up, examined it, and decided that it was no more interesting than any number of other rocks he had found in his life. It was, in fact, just a rock, and pretty boring. He tossed it away, then spied a crow sunning itself twenty feet off and wished he'd kept the rock to throw at the crow.

The sun over his right shoulder made it about three o'clock. He could go down to Brant Oakey's smithy, pinch a couple of horseshoe nails, and put them, one crossed over the other, on the railroad tracks. If he did it right, the train would weld them into a tiny pair of scissors. However, he'd never managed to do it right before, and there was little to encourage him about its happening on this weary day.

He could go see Billy Toback, and maybe the two of them could wheedle a chunk of ice from the iceman. But Billy Toback had called him a crapface yesterday, and sulking about that colossal insult was really more satisfying than making up with Billy.

He could go home and look in the stereograph at the fifty views of the daily routine in the H.J. Heinz pickling works that an eastern cousin had inexplicably sent his family. Or he could set off the single cannon cracker that still lay fat and potent in his dresser drawer, left over from the Fourth. Or he could read one of the dime novels he wasn't allowed to own, but did. Or he could go to the creek and find a crayfish which, once pounded to pieces, might yield up a couple of the small white disks that were such effective good-luck pieces.

He had just reached the post road when he heard the noise of harness and turned to see a surrey coming his way. He recognized it at once: the best carriage Nat Welder's livery stable could offer, a flashy rig with the lacquer so deep on its sides that it looked wet. Winton Reese, whose father owned the Merchants' Bank, was at the reins and next to him was Betty Langdon, who everybody knew was Tom Dunn's girl.

"Jemmy, why, Jemmy Stockholm," she called. "Now, stop, Winton, and let's see if Jemmy wants a ride home. Aren't you perishing, Jemmy?"

"It's hot," Jemmy said. Reese reined in the horses. He looked mad about something. Jemmy shot up into the surrey before Betty could change her mind.

"Hello, Jemmy," said Betty. She had a lot of pink in her cheeks and she looked mad, too, even though she was smiling and being pleasant. "You've been picking raspberries, haven't you?"

"Yes'm," said Jemmy. "I got a bunch of them for my mother and she says I can sell the ones she doesn't use. Would you like some?" He offered her the bucket, then added, "You don't have to pay."

"Why, thank you." She put two or three berries in her mouth. She was a very pretty woman. With her high color and shiny dark hair she looked to Jemmy like a girl in a sarsaparilla advertisement. "Why, they're just delicious," she said. "Where did you get them?"

"In the clearing about a mile back that way," said Jemmy, surprised and pleased by the amount of attention she was giving him. "There's thousands more."

"These are just right. Another two or three days and they'd be overripe, but now they're perfect. If it weren't so hot I'd go after some myself."

"Take some more. I've got lots."

She turned to Reese and said in an altogether different tone of voice, "Would you care for some?"

Reese muttered.

"What did you say, Winton?" she asked.

"I said, to hell with Jemmy's goddamned berries."

Jemmy was astounded to hear a grown-up say something like that in front of a woman. He was boy enough to be a little hurt by what he took as an insult directed at his berries, but old enough, too, to realize that this was something that had started before he got in the surrey. At any rate the listless summer day was suddenly charged with event.

Betty turned back to him; the bridge of her nose looked white and pinched; otherwise she might have been responding to a bit of good-humored stubbornness on Reese's part as she said, "I don't know what's the matter with Winton, Jemmy. Just a little while ago he was being friendlier than you'd believe. Don't let him bother you," she went on with relentless good cheer. "I'm very glad for your company and I know your mother will make some wonderful jam out of those berries."

She talked to Jemmy, not giving Winton so much as a glance while they rolled toward town. The dust they raised hung motionless in the air behind them.

They were a block away from Jemmy's house when he saw the box wagon parked in front of it. "Aw," he said. As he watched, the huge wagon box tipped up and spilled out a daunting heap of firewood. Four hours' work, at least, he calculated, to get it all stacked out back.

"I'll get off here," he said quickly. "Thanks for the ride."

Betty said good-bye as he swung down off the surrey holding his pail of berries. If he stayed out until dinnertime he might not have to stack the wood until tomorrow. He cut across the Crogans' yard, making for Billy Toback's house, eager to tell Billy about how Winton Reese said "goddamned" and "hell" to Betty Langdon.

"You certainly have a nice gentle way with children, Winton," Betty said after Jemmy had scampered away. "But I'm surprised you didn't offer him some whiskey after you were finished cursing at him."

Reese produced a sarcastic laugh. "Hawr. Hawr. Hawr." It was a staple in his limited supply of rhetorical tricks and, though shopworn and mechanical, it was enough to enrage her. Hoping for a wearily olympian tone, she said, "You're such a tiresome bounder."

But Reese had seen his laugh strike home. "You shouldn't lead men on if you don't like the results."

"Oh!" Betty glared at him. "Lead you on!"

She started to utter a sarcastic laugh of her own, struggled against it, and had a sudden fierce vision of how appalled Reese would be if she spat in his smirking face. Her immediate shock at the violent impulse checked her mounting anger long enough for a cool, rueful thought to slip through: He's right—I did lead him on, and that's why I'm so mad.

She hadn't led him on much, of course, and wouldn't have led him on at all if it weren't for Tom Dunn. And the worst of it was that the ugly afternoon probably wouldn't stir Tom up anyway. Not much did.

Two years had passed since Betty had given up telling herself that Tom was nothing special. She knew it and it didn't make a bit of difference. She could have had men as well off as Winton Reese, and far less odious, but she just didn't want them. She wanted Tom Dunn, a railroad telegrapher; she would have wanted him if he were a beggar, and that was that. It was a condition of her life, less trying, she supposed, than asthma would have been.

Betty had met Tom when she moved to Hinckley the summer she was sixteen. Her father had taken a job as manager of the brand-new Wilbur Hotel, and he brought Betty and her mother north from St. Paul, to the consternation of a good many Hinckley girls. For Betty, at sixteen, was beautiful. Her photographs didn't show it: stiffened and solemn for the camera, she had a sharp chin and too much mouth, and eyes set fat apart over high, almost Asian cheekbones. But even her expostulations of dismay over the photographs belied the drab images. Her face was always in motion, her mouth generous and amused, her eyes dark blue-green with hot little points of gold in them.

She had been pretty all her life and she was easy with it: she carried herself, cheerful and alert, through a month of venom from the local girls, most of them spurred to their wrath by Julia McKinney, who for years had been secure in her position as the prettiest girl in school. Betty didn't care because soon there were half a dozen boys gathering on her porch in the evenings to drink strawberry lemonade and listen to Clyde Bricklow play his mandolin. The girls boycotted Betty's porch for a few weeks, but that was where the boys were, and by September the more pragmatic had given in. Finally, even the usurped Julia McKinney deigned to make an appearance at Betty's Halloween party.

Tom Dunn came by from time to time although he preferred to spend his evenings at the depot. Already his friends were beginning to patronize him for that. When they were ten, all of them had wanted to be either railroad men or baseball players, but at sixteen they were starting to consider more realistic careers. Clyde Bricklow, who thought he was all the candy, was more precocious than most with his early avowed purpose to "make a barrelful of money in Lakes shipping."

Betty first became aware of Tom as something more than a quiet peripheral figure that winter, at a taffy pull. She gave a lot of parties—Halloween, Thanksgiving, Christmas—all at her parents' urging. Both her mother and father were timid people, gray, spectacled, and tidy, who had met late in life and were proud and baffled to have produced such a vivid daughter. Neither had had many friends when they were young, and both were convinced that the only way to ensure a happy life for Betty was constantly to stage what her mother called "nice little entertainments."

The entertainments involved weeks of preparation, for each had to have a theme. At Thanksgiving, for instance, Betty's mother, scrupulously following the instructions in *Ackerman's Universal Guide to Party-Giving*, had braided a dozen cornucopias out of straw and filled them with chocolates and—a stunning rarity—oranges. Betty helped her mother hang Indian corn, wrote out the invitations, put watercolors on the cut of the big turkey-cock in *Harper's Weekly*, and hung it on the wall. Her father stood by blinking behind his glasses, rubbing his hands together, and saying, from time to time, "It's going to be quite a shivaree."

When the party finally occurred, Betty rushed around making sure everybody was having fun and took care to pause and smile at her mother, who stood flushed and wistful in the shadow of the tall Dutch grandfather clock. She endured the inevitable game of charades, in which, to her misery, she was stuck with acting out "How can man die better / Than facing fearful odds / For the ashes of his fathers / And the temples of his gods?" while the crowd shouted out "Sleep?" "Tub?" "Blizzard?" "Cow?" And when the last guest had gone noisy into the cold night, Betty's mother said, as she always said, "Didn't you enjoy it, dear?" and Betty exclaimed as she always exclaimed, "Oh, yes!"

The Christmas party came and went, and then the New Year's

party. Betty had thought she was off the hook until Washington's Birthday, and had to reach to summon the necessary pleasure when her mother announced the taffy pull.

It was deep winter, the snow fine and gritty as sand on the ground, the wind knifing down barely blunted by Hinckley's low wooden buildings and the thousands of miles of New World pine forest that stood between the taffy pullers and the tumbled arctic icescapes where the wind was born. Clyde Bricklow stood in the lee of the house, swatting at his mandolin and singing "Why Did They Dig Ma's Grave So Deep?" in a tragic voice while the rest of them pulled the gummy, steaming candy into long white strands and dropped it in the snow. It melted a trough for itself, then hardened.

"It's taffy, it's taffy!" cried Winette Beal, and Betty, ever the good hostess, clapped her hands and shrieked, "It is indeed!"

A quiet voice beside her said, "And here I'd been expecting rhubarb."

She looked up from her joyful examination of the taffy to see Tom Dunn standing, hands in his pockets, quiet under the winter constellations.

She hadn't spoken to him once that evening, and not much before; she bore him no ill will, but he never had anything to say. A seventeen-year-old boy with a pleasant, squarish face who still liked railroads. Now he seemed to be making fun of her. Maybe not.

"Why, Tom, I hope you're having a good time."

He shrugged. "Better than you, anyway."

It was one thing to do through evenings like this—it was another to be baited about it by a cipher like Tom Dunn. "I don't know what you're talking about," she said.

"Maybe not. But I'll bet you give a lot more parties than you'd like to. It always seems like you're doing a job of work, like a good actress."

Clyde had shifted to "The Widow Nolan's Goat," and this humorous favorite had drawn others over to him, leaving Betty and Tom by themselves in the corner of the yard.

"Well, thank you for saying I'm good, anyway. The best compliment a girl can get is to be able to pull a boy away from the roundhouse for an evening."

Tom smiled. "Oh, I just come to hear Clyde Bricklow sing the same four songs and tell the same ten jokes. He's even better than you—same show every night. That's real acting."

Betty giggled, and quickly put her hand to her mouth. It wasn't for her to laugh at her guests. "Clyde's a great addition to the group," she said primly, and wondered if the stiff phrase had come out of *Ackerman*'s.

Tom laughed. "Song's over. Now he'll start with his Hebe jokes." Sure enough. A frantic Teutonic accent came across the yard to them as Clyde began his round of jokes about Jewish merchants burning down their stores for the insurance. They made Betty uncomfortable; everybody told jokes like that, but the only Jew she'd ever seen was Isaac Guest, a sad, pleasant man who came to town twice a year in a cluttered wagon selling tinware.

". . . So Paddy says, 'Oi think it was an *Israel*-light started the foire, yer honor.' "

"Wonderful," said Tom, "just as good as ever."

"What's wrong with it?" said Betty lamely, irked at defending Clyde.

"Oh, nothing, I suppose. But here's Clyde talking day in and day out about how he's going to make a pile of money, and then telling jokes about how greedy Jews are. You ever see Ike Guest burn down his cart?"

Betty nearly asked Tom how he knew she was thinking about Ike Guest. Instead, she said, "Clyde doesn't mean any harm."

"I guess not," said Tom. "Say, shouldn't we be getting back inside?"

"You're absolutely right," Betty said. She ran across the yard calling, with angry gaiety, "Everybody indoors before we all freeze to death."

That night she lay in her bed with the wind rattling dry snow against the window and went over her conversation with Tom. From her point of view, it had been wholly unsatisfactory; someone had come along and said perspicacious things about her, and she had responded by sounding like a mean-spirited ninny. Well, at least it showed he had been watching her. She smiled. The still, cold snow light bloomed in the room around her, and she went to sleep listening to the stove pop and chatter to itself in the parlor below.

Two days later she walked home from school with Lucy Bateson, a tall, awkward girl who had gained a certain exasperated generosity of spirit by growing up the only sister of six brothers. Lucy was complaining about the impossibility of keeping the kitchen livable under this fraternal siege when Tom Dunn loped past, shouting a greeting.

"Say, Tom," called Lucy, "come on back and tell us a railroad story. We're dying to hear a good railroad story."

Tom turned, trotted backwards for a few paces, grinning. "I could tell you a dandy about changing a flat pilot wheel on a Mogul, but I'm late at the store. My father'll have a fit." He waved and ran on.

The sun blazed through a rip in the clouds and for a moment everything was a blinding wet dazzle. Betty heard Lucy say, "Tom Dunn's nice. And he's sweet on you."

"Oh, he isn't either," said Betty quickly. The sun went away; the street became again a trough of winter murk.

"Is too," said Lucy. "So's my brother Will, but he's too shy ever to show it. Wish he wasn't. Wish he'd come over and spill food in your kitchen for a change."

"I don't believe it about Tom. He didn't say anything to you, did he?"

"Yes, he did."

"What? What did he say?"

"I shouldn't tell."

"Stop it. You tell me."

"He said that how they keep track of freight cars is with lots of little notes—waybills, I think he called them—and each time a train comes in a man takes them and—"

"I hope your brother butchers a goat in the kitchen," said Betty.

Lucy nudged her. "Look what's coming," she said quietly just as Betty saw Tom heading back their way.

He explained to the girls that when he'd passed the clock in the confectioner's window, he found it was earlier than he'd thought, and could walk along with them for a ways after all.

"What a shame," said Lucy, "for I just this minute remembered something I left at school."

She ran off, leaving Betty fiercely embarrassed by the transparent ploy. Tom laughed as though Lucy had just said something exceptionally witty. Betty found herself tugging at his sleeve. "Listen," she said, low, quick, and hard, "I don't like Clyde Bricklow, I don't like his jokes, and I give parties 'cause my parents want me to, if it's any business of yours."

Tom mumbled something.

"What?"

"Nothing."

"What?"

"Walk you home?"

Shocked by her own forwardness, Betty started out in silence and Tom, who had been so easy and ironic during the taffy pull, was apparently abashed by the boldness of his invitation. He walked with glum purpose, hands sunk in his pockets, puffing white breath down at his chest. She stepped along gaily, smiling, looking up at the pale empty sky and down at the pale empty ground as though a balloon ascension and a sulky race were vying for her attention. Neither of them said a word.

At last the sound of the 4:15's whistle blew down on them and Tom burst into a baffling story about railroad telegraphy. Betty hung on every word.

The desperate telling and listening ebbed as they passed the Adams Express office and turned toward Betty's house. At last, even though they were still four houses away from Betty's, Tom said, "I've liked the walk."

"So have I, Tom," Betty said and then, quickly, "How do you come to know so much?"

"Oh, you know, I work with Sy, and there's not much he doesn't know about brass pounding."

"I meant about me. What you said during the taffy pull."

She was afraid he would pretend he didn't know what she meant, but he answered instantly. "I guess I just watch you. I guess I have since you got here. You're a deal more interesting than Julia McKinney. Not that she'd care what I thought."

Betty, happier that she'd been since she moved to Hinckley, wished for two minutes' grace to think of something to say in reply, but they were already climbing the three gray-painted steps of her house. She reached for the front door at the same time Tom did, and it wasn't awkward at all: he just bent down right there in the winter dusk and kissed her on the corner of her mouth, so that it kept buzzing softly in her cheek as he ran off down the steps and she went in to help her mother with supper.

It was a fine beginning, but nothing much came of it. Tom continued to seek her out, but not very diligently. Occasionally he walked her home, but he didn't kiss her again. Once in a while he showed traces of the sympathetic irony that had drawn her during the taffy pull, but for the most part he was merely quiet and pleasant.

Betty wasn't like the heroines in the novels she sometimes read; Tom hadn't stolen her heart away with a kiss. She knew about kissing. A pretty girl gets kissed. She'd even been kissed by Clyde Bricklow in a fast, confident, bloodless way. But somehow Tom had gotten under her skin.

The others sensed it, and gradually boys who had been paying more or less open court to her drifted off to find more amenable companions. So she was left, finally, with someone who treated her with an offhand, distracted good nature that would have been delightful in an older brother but was increasingly tiresome in a beau. Betty was not a sentimentalist. She didn't want a lot of ardent gush. But she wanted something more than the occasional ice cream soda from a great chum who could always be counted on for a crackling good railroad yarn in between songs at the band concert.

Once, and once only, she did get something more. She had awakened very early one morning into a muggy, wretched day. The sun wasn't yet up; the flat gray light barely showed the loom of her dresser and washstand. She was lying, cross and sweaty, willing herself back to sleep when she heard her name being called, so softly that at first she thought she had got to sleep after all, and was dreaming.

Holding her nightdress closed under her chin, she leaned out the window and saw Tom standing in the dim yard.

"Betty," he called in a hoarse, dry whisper, "Betty, please come down here."

She shook her head. "What are you doing? Everybody's asleep."

"Betty, please come down. It's important."

"I can't, Tom. Can't it wait till after breakfast?"

"Jesus Christ, Betty, will you come down here?"

She hesitated a moment, alarmed and curious. "All right." There was no time to get dressed and her hair was probably a horror, but if Tom was going to come for her in the middle of the night, he could take what he got.

She went quietly down the stairs, the steps feeling strange and oily under her bare feet, and past the parlor which, oddly, was feeding a current of cool air into the close hall like an underground spring.

Tom was waiting by the porch when she stepped outside.

"Betty, I'm sorry but—"

"What are you doing up so early?"

"I've had the key all night. Sy got drunk and put a freight on the track with the limited. He just cleared the freight, and off she went."

"Tom, did you get me out here to tell me a railroad story? Are you crazy?"

"No, Betty, listen, there was a big wreck. People are dead."

"Oh." He looked gaunt and tired and scared. "Oh, Tom. When?"

"Last night, about eleven, during the storm. Then he ran off, and I took the key."

"But it wasn't your fault? It was Sy's fault, wasn't it?"

"I could have stopped him. I could have stopped him if I'd been paying better attention. But once he let the freight go, there was nothing to do about it. I just sat there, and knew there was a train full of people and a lot of them going to be killed, and I knew it, and they didn't."

"Tom," Betty said in a flat, practical voice, "you couldn't have done a thing. Sy's the telegrapher. You can't go grabbing the key away from him every time you think he's doing something wrong. It's his job, not yours. I don't see there was a thing you could do. I just think it's wonderful that you were good enough to take over from him when he ran. You should be proud of yourself."

Tom listened, jiggling anxiously on one foot, then on the other.

When Betty was finished he said, "I don't know. I could have stopped him," so she guessed he wanted to hear it over again.

She went through her defense in three or four different ways with the spongy ground steaming fog around them, and then Tom took her by the shoulders and started kissing her hard on the mouth. After a while he pulled away and said stupidly, "You're not wearing anything underneath," and she laughed, asked him if he thought she slept in party dresses, and kissed him again. She felt a faint prod of guilt, not because of the kissing, but because she was ruthless enough to be grateful for the train wreck. Tom was nuzzling at her neck and stroking her breasts when her mother called from the porch.

There were no other mornings—or evenings—like that one. After Tom got over the wreck, he became as bland and circumspect as ever. Several times, sitting alone on her front porch in the evening, she decided not to see him again. But always, after an angry, wakeful night, she wearily conceded to herself that she was stuck and had to wait out his shyness or indifference or propriety or whatever it was. She had to be patient.

Patient she was, brushing away her parents' timid inquiries with harsh good humor, and seeing Tom whenever he chose. But she wasn't quite patient enough to turn down Winton Reese when he came to her door in a new suit and asked her to go for a buggy ride.

Betty didn't know Winton Reese very well and didn't like what she knew. Winton's father sent him East to be educated, and he showed up in town only at Christmastime and during the summer. He owned a two-hundred-dollar Columbia bicycle, and occasionally went scorching along Hinckley's main street; the rest of his time he devoted to being elegantly dressed and languid.

Nevertheless, he was a man, and a highly presentable one, and it wouldn't do any harm to have Tom hear that somebody still found her attractive. And Tom would hear; you could count on news like that getting around Hinckley with a celerity that beggared the Western Union cable.

She decided to go the moment Winton asked her, but paltered a minute for form's sake. "Why, Winton, this is such a surprise. I'm terribly busy, but . . . Well, it is so hot, it would be lovely to get out . . .

Yes, yes . . . I'd like that. Here, you can talk to Mother while I get ready." This would give her parents, who were obviously puzzled and dismayed by the solitary prominence Tom had gained in her life, something to chew on. Everything seemed to be working to her advantage, and maybe she'd even enjoy the ride.

She didn't. The moment Winton handed her up into the surrey he said, "Charming woman, your mother."

"Why, thank you," said Betty, trying to imagine Tom calling anything "charming."

Winton shook the reins, the horse stirred itself into a somnolent lope, and, with no preamble whatever, Winton launched into a series of stories so self-aggrandizing they took her breath away.

It was marvelous, going East to school, gave a fellow a certain polish. Oh, they could be snobby there, but Winton was so smooth that he was rapturously welcomed in drawing rooms from Newport to Philadelphia. The beautiful women back East tended to be a bit chilly and holier-than-thou, but Winton could take his pick of the lot of them. "I find they all go for me, sooner or later," was how he phrased it. Then, in what Betty guessed was a nod to the conventions of modesty, he added, "I just don't know what it is about me." She didn't know either, so she kept her mouth shut, and tried for a plausible smile.

As they passed the Brennan Lumber Company, Winton shifted his emphasis away from women to more general triumphs. Betty sat inside her smile and decided this was a steep price to pay to prod Tom.

Beyond Grindstone Creek the pines closed in around the road, and they rattled along under a covering of sere, scrawny branches. Before long they came to a clearing, a scruffy patch of enervated weeds. A derelict rowboat, its timbers bleached bone white, lay at the edge of the clearing, suggesting that at some unimaginable time there had been water there. Winton dropped the reins and said "Ahhh" in an awed tone, as though he'd brought Betty to a cerulean lake outside of Lucerne. Then he displayed some of the charm that had melted the ice maidens of the stuffy old East.

He turned to Betty, put one hand on the small of her back, one on her right breast, and thrust his tongue into her throat. He moved with the speed of thought, and for a stupefied moment Betty sat there, still smiling around his tongue. Then she slapped him. There was nothing coquettish about the slap; she moved her arm stiff from the shoulder and put all the force she could muster into it. Winton yelped and jumped away, hand over his mouth.

"You . . . you made me bite my tongue."

"Well, you shouldn't have tried to bite mine. Take me home this second—" She paused, and added, "Winton Reese" simply because at that instant the name held for her all the loathing she wished to express.

Winton, livid, reined the horse around and they left the enchanted glade and headed back toward town. Betty stared straight ahead while Winton dabbed blood from his mouth with a handkerchief.

"I could have been severely injured," he said after a while.

"You wouldn't have been injured at all if you had kept your hands to yourself."

"I simply fail to understand you tank town girls. There's nothing in a little kiss."

"Save it for Consuelo Vanderbilt."

Winton was beginning another rebuke when Betty spied Jemmy Stockholm and called him into the surrey.

The woods had been hot enough, but Hinckley seemed positively infernal by comparison, the buildings parched and dwindled in the palpable air.

"Please let me off here," said Betty as they approached the St. Paul & Duluth depot.

Winton gave his sarcastic laugh; this, Betty vowed, would be the last time in her life she would hear it. He didn't get out to help her down, and as she stepped to the street he said, "I daresay your telegraph friend will have a fine time tonight, now I've warmed you up for him."

Betty smiled up at him. "Thank you for a lovely ride."

Winton drove off. The air filled with wind and whirring; soft, heavy things bounced against her. She screamed and stumbled, and someone grabbed her by the waist and held her upright as something thumped against her face, tumbled by it with a harsh, frantic thrumming. Wings. Birds.

They were gone; she looked down the street to see a dozen of them whip around the corner of the Williams Hotel and out of sight. She turned to the person who had kept her from falling and saw a hot, tired-looking man of about thirty, with wrinkles around his eyes and a good, strong jaw.

"Who are you?" she asked, dazed, then remembered herself: "I mean, thank you. I would have fallen."

"I'm Scott Keegan. I'm a drummer, though you couldn't prove it by my recent performance. Birds like to fly through your town all the time?"

"I've never seen anything like it. They never come out of the woods that way."

"Something must have driven them out." He sniffed the air. "Anything burning around here?"

"Oh, it's always like this in the summer." Then, feeling a laggard spur of civic pride, Betty added, "Well, it's not always quite this bad. Sometimes it's very nice. But the farmers burn their lands to clear them and the lumbermen are always burning something, so sometimes, when it's hot, it get smoky."

"Everything's made of wood here," said Keegan.

"Oh, nothing ever happens. A barn burned up two years ago, but it was abandoned anyway."

Keegan shrugged.

"Well, I do thank you," said Betty. "Those birds surely took me by surprise."

"Don't thank me, just buy a lot of barber supplies."

Betty laughed. "Is that what you sell?"

"It's what I haven't been selling, recently. You'd think people had stopped getting haircuts."

"I'm sure things will pick up," Betty said. "Thank you again."

Keegan nodded and Betty started up the depot steps. Given the day she'd just endured, she wanted to see firsthand what effect her jaunt had on Tom.

But by the time she got to the door, she felt too spent and anxious to make a good showing. She could count on the Hinckley intelligence services to alert Tom to her day. He had said he'd be stopping by tonight, and he would certainly have heard by then. She turned away and walked down the steps. She would think of some things to say to Tom later; right now she wanted some milk, a nap, and a sponge bath.

Keegan watched Betty walk away from the depot. First good thing I've seen in Hinckley, he thought. Then he stepped into the barroom of the hotel and saw another. Like most traveling men, Keegan spent a fair amount of time in railroad hotel saloons, and he could judge them as soon as he stepped inside. This was a good one.

Windows along the walls let in the late afternoon daylight, but the tall mirror behind the bar threw its own light into the room, a placid silvery glow that took the edge off outdoor concerns. The wagons going by on the street outside made muted, companionable noises; the ceiling was high and stained with years of tobacco smoke; a small wooden Indian guarding a glass case indicated that you could buy a cigar right there, you didn't have to go into the lobby. The bartender came over at once.

"Yessir." Not yes, stranger. Not too familiar.

He'd had a bad afternoon and whiskey wouldn't be out of place. But it was so hot. "Beer, if it's cold."

The bartender turned and took a good, big schooner from the top of a shining pyramid. "Oh, it's cold. Wouldn't last long here if I sold warm beer."

Sure enough, Keegan knew it was cold even before he tasted it, felt it cool under his chin as he lifted the glass. The beer was dry, sharp, and altogether admirable; ice harvested up on the lakes last winter made it cold enough to hurt his teeth.

"Good," he said, wiping foam from his lip with the back of his hand.

The bartender looked pleased. "Made right down the line in St. Paul. Folks who know say it's good as Milwaukee."

Keegan, expansive, said, "It's better. I was in Milwaukee a week ago. Had some beer there that'd already gone through a horse."

The bartender laughed, delighted to get a compliment and a joke at the same time. Then he said, "Excuse me," and went to the far end of the bar to take care of three men who were deep in good-humored argument about who was best in the Hinckley Cornet Band. Keegan studied the two paintings above the bar who elaborate gold frames were hung with the same strange black fuzz that seemed to grow on every gold frame on every painting in every barroom in the nation. One was the obligatory nude, pillowy and at ease among ferns. The other was a Civil War scene that had the two armies meeting head on in a mutual charge. Every second man was carrying a flag, and nobody had got hurt. Next to the happy battle, a photograph nailed to the wall showed a team of horses pulling a sledge loaded with colossal logs over a snowy road. Someone had scrawled a frantic legend across the sky over the logs: "Biggest load of lumber! Ever brought out of the Woods! At Hinckley! Sent to the Great! Centennial! Exhibition! In Philadelphia Pennsylvania! Thousands Marveled—1876."

Keegan was smiling at the marvelous load of logs when a voice at his shoulder said, "You haven't paid for anything yet, have you?"

He turned to a beaming LeMoyne. "Well, yes, a dime."

"Pay no more. I'm buying tonight. What are you having? Beer? Have champagne."

"I don't like champagne. Why are you buying?"

"I've had a fine stroke of luck. I was down at the depot when a new fire engine came in. I saw my chance, started yapping, and sold eleven fire engine watches at seven fifty each. That's eighty-two fifty, which means I get forty-one twenty-five. Not bad for a half hour's work."

"Not bad," Keegan agreed. The bartender came over and LeMoyne ordered whiskey for himself, another beer for Keegan. "Anyway, I'll buy supper. I'm going to be ready to tuck into a steak. You think you can get a steak in this burg that's worth the trouble of eating it?"

The bartender took the challenge. "A course you can," he broke in, looking hurt. "Right here in this hotel you can get a steak worth two of that overpriced shoe leather they peddle up to Duluth. Oysters, too. We've got an oyster saloon even Easterners say is nonpareel."

"Non-what?" asked LeMoyne.

"Nonpareel. It means better than anything."

"Fine," said LeMoyne. "This is right where we'll eat, then. Always glad to get an inside line on where's good to eat in a town. I'm a traveling man and I'd've starved to death long ago without the good counsel of barkeeps like yourself. And, as you can see, starvation isn't threatening me right away. First thing I do when I hit a town is I seek out the best saloon, and ask . . ." Keegan watched, rueful and admiring, as LeMoyne slipped into a jovial harangue. In ten minutes he had sold the bartender a watch that had "Gambrinus" stamped on the back, and a chain with a gold keg for a fob. He winked at Keegan as the man signed the order form.

"You're pretty damned good," Keegan said after the bartender had gone off, eight dollars and thirty cents poorer.

"Ahh," said LeMoyne, "some days I'm hot, some days I'd do better to stay in bed. This is a good day. You have any luck?"

"Nope. My own fault, too. Misread a situation and came off like an ass. Actually had somebody throw a catalog at me."

LeMoyne laughed. "Well, drown your sorrows. Tomorrow's another day."

"Yeah," said Keegan. "You got a watch with a sample case and a sore foot on it?"

In an hour, Keegan was feeling better about his barren day. LeMoyne was a pleasantly officious host, urging more beer on him and ordering plate after plate of oysters, which were all the bartender had promised, fresh, briny, and sweet. Even the bathroom was excellent: a snowy bank of tall vitrified-enamel urinals, with businesslike slate slabs between them, so that they invited homely conversation between occupants.

He was returning from his third trip when LeMoyne put a vast hand on the small of his back and thrust him from the bar into the dining room, where a waiter set yet another plate of oysters on a tablecloth that was starched glassy. "Can't get enough oysters into you," said LeMoyne, "they're nothing but water and fizz. Never fill you up."

"Fizz?" asked Keegan.

"Oh, you know, fizz." LeMoyne smirked and dropped his voice into sputtering intimacy. "Make you able, if you take my meaning."

"Oh." Keegan saw him and LeMoyne at the table as in a distant photograph, stuff in leering complicity: two drummers talking women.

LeMoyne saw his face change. "Something the matter, Scott?" he asked, the bawdry leaving his tone. "What's wrong?" Keegan, moved by the nice bar or the clean dining room or the splendid urinals, or perhaps just by the old salesman's trick of using your first name, told him.

"You know, in the train this afternoon, when you said your wife wasn't pretty they way Jeanie Carron on the Tilton Circuit was pretty?"

"Say, now wait a minute. My wife is a mighty nice-looking—"

Keegan waved him quiet.

"What I meant was, it made me think of my wife, because Jeanie Carron was sitting right there at the table when I met her."

"No horse?" said LeMoyne, impressed.

"It's true, but Jeanie Carron wasn't such a much then. She wasn't even with Tilton yet. She was dancing with three other girls in a novelty quartet, and some of the Kraut and Dohnal boys took me to see her to celebrate my selling two thousand dollars' worth of equipment in one afternoon without leaving my desk in the main office."

LeMoyne whistled.

"Right. They came to me in those days. Anyway, the show was terrible. Even Jeanie Carron was terrible. But afterward we went to a café and had dinner with the girls we'd just seen.

"That's where I met Amy Quatt. She was small—much smaller than she'd looked onstage—and she was pretty. Kind, too, without being holy about it. I went back to the show the next day. In a week I asked her to marry me, but she said no, she didn't want to get married."

He began shredding a roll onto the tablecloth.

"A couple of weeks later I left the office and there was Amy waiting for me. She said the show'd folded, that Jeanie Carron and the owner had cut out with the money. She said she was owed a week's time, and she couldn't pay her boardinghouse, and she'd marry me if I still wanted to. Said she didn't know how good a wife she'd make, but she'd try her best.

"I rented us a pretty nice little house, fully furnished, and we had a good time. I had money then. We'd go out and see vaudeville shows and I'd bring her presents. She said she was happy."

"Sounds fine," LeMoyne said cautiously.

"It was. Then, after a year, Amy said her cousin Larry was coming to Chicago on business and could he stay with us? I said sure, and in a week a great big bastard in yellow shoes and a hundred-dollar suit came in the door with a steamer trunk you could drive a wagon into. Right away he started telling lame stories while Amy laughed fit to die. When he wasn't cutting his awful jokes, he was talking about making money trading jute. You know what jute is?"

LeMoyne shook his head. "Some kind of tree?"

Keegan shrugged. "I never knew either. And I was damned if I was going to ask Cousin Larry. I've always meant to find out, though.

"He stayed with us for about a week, and it wasn't too much fun. Amy thought I was making it too plain I didn't like him, so she was sore at me. I said I liked him fine. Then one Monday I was halfway to work when I remembered I'd left behind a list of stops I had to make. So I went back, and when I opened the door, there was Cousin Larry on the sofa, and Amy was with him."

"Holy God," LeMoyne said quietly, "that's rough sledding. I don't know what I'd do. It's just like"—he looked past Keegan into the world of nightmare burlesque where jokes were born, where his own wife might be surprised in the parlor with Cousin Larry—"I mean, it's just like the stories they tell on us."

Keegan nodded, remembering Cousin Larry saying "Goddamn" in a subdued, reverent voice and running up the stairs. Keegan had thought of going after him, but he just felt too tired. He turned and walked out the door and down the steps and up the street. It had been early autumn, and the trees were red and yellow, and the day bright as could be. He drank away a quick morning, a quick afternoon, and a long evening, through which he tottered from saloon to saloon while the flattened red sun hung a stubborn quarter inch above the horizon.

When he got home the next morning the house was still and empty, and strangely dusty, as though he'd been away a long time. Cousin Larry and his barn of a steamer trunk were gone, and Amy was gone. She hadn't left a note.

He spent the next night in a hotel. A week later, he was on the road.

It seemed to get hotter as it got darker. LeMoyne, flushed, sweaty, and sympathetic, had gone up to bed. But the good steak dinner lay solid in Keegan's stomach, and he'd unsettled himself by talking about Amy, and so he went out for a walk.

The night was absolutely still. On dark porches he could hear ice rattling in pitchers of lemonade. A single red light burned in the Adams Express Company, making the inside of the office look as hospitable as a furnace. He passed a bakery, and thought there were worse things than being a drummer: imagine being up before dawn, shoveling dough into an oven. The bank next to the bakery was made of wood. He wouldn't put his money in a wooden bank. In fact, he wouldn't have any money to put anywhere if things didn't pick up soon.

And, thinking that, he came to Albert Craid's barbershop. It was still lighted and Craid was sweeping out the last of the day's fall of hair. To his satisfaction, Keegan saw that the fixtures were far shabbier than those in the palace where he'd been humiliated that afternoon. Perhaps Craid would buy from him. For a moment he considered going in then and there, but he didn't have his sample case with him, he was tired, and he'd had enough of selling for one day. He moved along and came to the firehouse.

Inside the open door, he saw the firemen polishing the steam dome of the new engine, though it scarcely needed it. Damn, thought Keegan, but LeMoyne must have some kind of genius. Imagine him being right there on the station platform when that fire engine came in. Keegan had yet to step into a barbershop minutes after the town madman had smashed all the mugs and set the chairs on fire. He shook his head and walked on.

"I've got a name for her," Noble Barrett said, straightening up from waxing one of the wheels.

Chief Craig dropped the scrap of waste he'd been using to buff the dome. "What?"

"A name. For the engine."

"It's got a name. Waterous."

"No. I mean, we'll christen it. We'll call it the Hyperion."

"The hell we will. What's it mean, anyway?"

"It's a Greek god. A sun god. We'll put it on with gold leaf. We can get Ed Clayter to do it tomorrow."

"Look, Noble, you can call your drugstore any goddamned silly thing you choose. But I'm not going to give this engine some namby-pamby moniker."

"Think of it," Barrett persisted. "All in gold, maybe blue trim."

"How about some petticoats for the stack?"

Barrett snorted. "Should know better'n try out any elevated idea on a man who spits through his face."

"When we going to steam her up?" asked Tim Murray, who kept the stationery store.

"Tomorrow," said Craig. "We'll see if she works tomorrow."

Betty Langdon lay in her airless room and thought about her day with Winton Reese and about Tom Dunn, who hadn't come by after all, and wished that people reproduced the way amoebae did.

Jim Root, pulling out of Pokegama, followed the pale wash of his head lamp into the forest. Jack McGowan sprinkled some coal in the firebox, then sat and pulled his hat down over his eyes. This vision of the easy comforts of youth nettled Root; by this time of night the old engineer's elbow was shrilling even when he wasn't using his arm. He was casting about for something to stir up Jack with when they rounded a familiar bend and saw the trees sheared off close to the ground, covered with vines now, but still eloquent of old violence.

They'd been cut off clean by Charlie MacMonies' locomotive swinging like a door on its hinge against the nose of Deacon Wheeler's after the drunken son of a bitch of a brass pounder at Hinckley had cleared Charlie's freight and put the two trains on the same track.

Every time Root passed the spot his cab, usually as homey to him as his own kitchen, seemed alien and malicious, full of cruel iron lances ready to spear him just the way poor Deke Wheeler had been run through that night by his own injector handle.

Root's arm throbbed and he glanced at McGowan, dozing away oblivious to all the potential carnage around him. Hope he sees a real wreck soon, Root thought brutally. He was immediately ashamed of himself, and then they were coming up on Hinckley. He pulled the whistle cord and Jack yawned and reached for his shovel. As they rolled into the depot, Root saw a couple of barrels and an empty baggage cart brushed with orange light from the bay window and young Tom Dunn, hand on the key, watching them come in.

Tom Dunn cleared Root, angry and exhausted. Sam Pollard, the night man, had sent word that he'd be around a little late. Tom had covered for him for five hours, and now he'd shown up with tragedy etched on his narrow scholar's face. "It's the runs, Tom," he said somberly. "I've got 'em something fierce. At first I was just a little griped, you know how it is, but then it came on and it burned and was thin as milk. Like hot milk, you know, when I—"

Tom rose from his chair, stretched enormously. "Sam, stop. I'm sorry, but I've had the key for fourteen hours straight and I really don't want to hear about it. If you'd come at six, I'd have listened like a doctor. But it's just too late."

Sam looked hurt. "If that's how you feel, but I think it's quite something I'm here at all. I thought you'd be glad to see me."

"I am, Sam. Goodnight."

Sam sat at the key. "Don't know what I'll do if it comes on again."

Tom walked out into the stultifying night, taking mean satisfaction in the thought of Sam stuck at the key when it came on again.

Toward midnight a blunt, dry breeze came up. Keegan felt it against his face as he mounted the steps to the hotel. It was parched and tepid and sour, but it meant the air was moving. Maybe tomorrow would be cooler.

He went up to his room, splashed blood-temperature water from his basin onto his face, took off his trousers and jacket, and lay on his back on the bed. His skin prickled and he felt angry.

Ten, fifteen minutes passed and he got up and turned off the gas mantle. He went back to bed and watched the curtains hanging stiff as tin and wondered what had happened to the breeze.

The last train had gone through two hours ago. Sam Pollard nodded at the key and brooded about his bowels. The firemen said goodnight to each other and left their engine with its grand smell of new paint and brass polish and canvas hose. The spokes were still green under their varnish; the wheels creaked and settled by minute degrees. Betty Langdon went to sleep and dreamed a dull hot dream of ironing small pieces of cloth. Jemmy Stockholm twitched and spun in his bed, rilled sweat, nearly fell to the floor, and slept dreamless throughout.

While they slept, the breeze Keegan had felt came back. It flowed hot and steady through the forest, blowing small fire into large ones. Smoldering stumps sent up thick flames, spilled sparks into the slash. Low, thick banks of smoke rolled out of the woods, over the lumber camps, into the town. Behind them, a hundred fires moved forward beneath the huge, close sky of Minnesota summer, crooked red fuses in the night.

September 1

Dustin Emmons woke from a dream that might have been more memory than dream—he was pushing seventy, and it was hard for him to tell, sometimes, whether he had been sleeping or not. It had been a simple dream, but there was great pleasure in it: he had been standing by the well of the house in Bucksport, Maine, where he'd been born, drinking cool water from a ladle while his mother said, "That's good, Dustin, that's good." He had not looked on her face for fifty years, but there she'd been, saying, "That's good."

Emmons rubbed his eyes; it was time to be up and about. He was bull cook for the Brennan Lumber Company camp Number Nine, and he had to be up earlier than anybody. Cruel Jimmy Bean, another old state of Maine man, lay snoring in the next bunk, rasping and twitching and clenching his fists; Emmons had never known a man to make such a job out of sleeping. Cruel Jimmy was one of the saw filers; Emmons bunked in their shack, so he wouldn't wake the jacks when he went out to stoke the stoves on winter nights. Cruel Jimmy made a series of droll little farting noises with his mouth, then slapped the top of his head and flopped over on his stomach. "Bub bub bub," he said.

Most of the men in camp neither knew nor cared where Cruel

Jimmy had gotten his nickname, but Emmons remembered. It had been back in the white-water days on the Saginaw. There'd been a log-jam, the black wet trunks looming and shifting, just about ready to let go, and a young Wisconsin jack with his hand caught between two of them, screaming and crying and ten seconds away from death. Jimmy Bean had danced out across the heaving logs, looked at the caught man for an instant with the lumber on the far shore already starting to give, and, with one quick, short stroke of his ax, cut off the man's hand right above the wrist. Then he tossed the jack, who had fainted straightaway, over his shoulder like a sack of flour and made it back to the bank, walking on water most of the way, as far as Emmons could tell.

Emmons stretched and coughed. It was close in the shack, and Cruel Jimmy smelled like a horse blanket. He stepped around the sleeping man and went out the door. It was close outside, too. Seemed darker than usual, but it was always pretty dark when he got up, so it was hard to tell.

He walked to the bunkhouse, stepped into the rough, close smell of thirty sleeping men, and went down between the rows of bunks, lighting the kerosene lamps. He took no pains to be quiet about it; the men would sleep as long as they could, and his puttering wouldn't waken them. He checked the barrel of water next to the washup sink and swapped a gray towel for the black one that hung next to the soap. You could put an edge on an ax with that chunk of soap. The wash-basins could be cleaner, but they'd do for the morning. He'd get to them after breakfast.

He went out the back of the bunkhouse and headed for the kitchen, gathered up a load of woof for the ranges, and went inside.

"Mornin', Dustin," said Dan Chite, the cookee.

"Mornin', Dan. What'll it be this mornin'? I know the men'd be surprised and happy if you made your famous sowbelly and beans."

Dan was easily baited. "Hey. Hey, now. They been bellyaching about my breakfast? They can goddamn well go over to Number Seven and eat the shit they dish out there. Don't I always get pork chops on Saturday? Don't I?"

"That what those are?" Emmons set down the wood. "I'll be

damned. The boys always just guessed they were sowbelly fritters."

"And don't they get biscuits? Every morning?"

"Every morning," Emmons conceded.

"And look at that wood you brought me. How can I bake right with that?"

"Best I could come up with."

Chite fed the wood into the range, then propped open the skylight above it.

"Smoky out this morning," he said.

"It's always smoky, this time of year," said Emmons.

But as he left the kitchen, and the cook began his ritual morning chant to rouse the sleeping jacks—"Get up, get up, get up—dyin' old Christ, ain't you gonna get up?"—Emmons heard a noise he'd never heard before. He had started lumbering in Calais, Maine, in time to see the eastern forests disappear, and had helped push the big clearing west all the way to Minnesota, and his life had been the life of the lumber camps. He knew every sound and smell there was in the camps, but this was new: a strange, ropy, heaving noise.

He followed the sound to its source; it was the horses. The smoke was so thick that they were coughing.

The whole dumb weight of the whole dumb summer, pressing down on Jemmy Stockholm's thin boy's chest, woke him. But he lay on his damp sheets feeling happy. He remembered his torpedo boat, which had come last Christmas in a slick red and cream box, with a picture on top that showed the craft, spare as a needle, cutting in against a huge enemy battle cruiser while a ten-year-old gunnery officer turned from his binoculars to shout information to the bridge. Hostile fire had built stiff white columns in the sea around the torpedo boat, but the lithe, lovely craft was unharmed and the bluejackets smiled as they fed shells into the bow gun under the boy officer's direction.

Then Jemmy remembered what had been in the box, and the mood and logic of summer returned to him. The boat—small, fragile, and tinny—lay on the windowsill with the dark green paint scabbing off its sides. It had been gathering dust there since New Year's Day;

after a week of glum, obligatory playing with it, Jemmy had put it aside as soon as he felt he could get away with it. Disgusted with the flimsy warship, he had nonetheless wanted to protect his parents from his scorn.

He'd protected them so well they'd never noticed it, and that made him sad. He lay on his muggy bed, waking up slowly, full of angry pity for his parents who didn't even know he hated the fine present they'd given him.

He glanced at the torpedo boat; it looked dim and slightly fuzzy. He was starting to go blind. The world was full of incomprehensible laws, and the penalties for breaking them were swift and harsh.

He blinked, but the dingy boat wouldn't draw itself into focus. Nothing in the room looked right. A bug landed delicately on his forehead. He slapped it, didn't feel anything, looked at his hand, and saw a gray streak. Ash. And now he remembered smoke and the smell of smoke, remembered it from his smoky sleep.

He got out of bed and padded to the window. As he approached it the boat took on its meager proportions. Reassured, he looked out into the backyard, saw the privy and the woodshed and the Crastons' house looking dim and strange the way the boat had. Smoke, fainter than fog, lay between the ground and the close sky, a sky the color of the dead-looking skin on a frog's belly.

So that was all. He started to whistle "Turkey in the Straw"—the best part of the summer had been discovering he could make a wonderful undulating noise by wobbling the back of his throat when he whistled—while he picked up his clothes from the floor. Then he remembered the unstacked firewood from yesterday. His brief pleasure at escaping blindness disappeared straightaway; his misery was complete.

The first mill whistle of the day hadn't sounded, so his parents wouldn't be up yet, nor would his sister, Edith, who had a better coverlet on her bed than he did just because she was a girl. Someday he'd be dead, and then they'd be sorry they made him do everything and loved his sister more. On his way downstairs he had a satisfying vision of his coffin being committed to the dry summer earth while his sorrowing parents realized how they'd taken him for granted. Then they'd go home and the neighbors would come by and tell them what a good boy he had been, and then his sister would have to carry the wood around back and stack it.

He went out through the stormshed, shouldered the yoke with a bucket on each end that his father had made for him, and walked to the pump. The handle creaked and the iron throat made its hollow, musical reaching noise, spat out a trickle of water, and then sent out a good solid stream—the envy of the neighborhood—which filled a pail with three strokes of the handle. Jemmy dragged the buckets back to the kitchen and emptied them into the stove reservoir. It was a big stove, all bound up in nickel, and it drank an unbelievable amount of water every morning. Sometimes Jemmy thought it was secretly connected to the boilers of the Brennan mill engines.

When he came back from his last trip, his mother was in the kitchen lighting the stove.

"Morning, Jemmy," she said, and reached down on her way to the icebox to irritate him with a kiss.

"I brought in all the water," he said bravely.

"Remember, it's Saturday."

The full injustice of it all settled on him. "I'll bring in enough water for everyone else, but I don't need a bath. It's not fair. If you want me to have a bath, then you should—"

"Careful, Jemmy." His mother smiled at him but he could tell she wasn't really interested. "Your father wouldn't like to hear you've been insolent."

That was true. His father had never once enjoyed his insolence. "I wasn't being insolent," he said.

"No, but you were about to be, and I saved you at the last moment. Now go stack that wood by way of thanking me."

"Aw, before breakfast? You never make me do chores before breakfast. I might get sick with no breakfast."

"I'm making pancakes." She scooped flour into a heavy brown bowl.

"What's that got to do with it?"

"Jemmy." She was angry now. He ran down the hall, went out

through the front door, and studied the pile of wood. It stood as high as he did. "Goddamn a snake fanny," he whispered. It was an oath Billy Toback had taught him. Then he picked up a single piece of wood and, cradling it in his arms, brought it around back.

"Hiho, Jemmy," his father called through the kitchen window, full of bestial grown-up cheer. "Don't kill yourself. Maybe you should have cut that in half before you tried to lift it."

"Good morning, Father," Jemmy said with dignity.

"Good morning, your grace," his father yelled back. "Breakfast's in five minutes."

Jemmy thought of saying he had too bad a bellyache to eat. A dozen convincing symptoms occurred to him immediately. But all they'd do would be to look it up in *Doctor Garnett's Complete Home Medical Encyclopaedia* and then give him something disgusting from a brown bottle. And, like as not, he'd end up getting no breakfast and still have to carry the wood. "Awright," he said.

The next trip he loaded his arms with wood until he couldn't see over the top of the stack, then lurched toward the backyard, puffing and grumbling as he passed under the kitchen window. He ran back, jolted another immense bundle into his arms, and tacked toward the pile on shaking legs.

On the fourth or fifth trip, his father called from the window, "Breakfast on the table, Jemmy."

He gasped and nodded as he tottered by, not about to squander his effect. He dumped the load, then returned to the window. "Father," he said when he'd caught his breath, "I'd prefer to finish my chore before breakfast."

"Your chore'll finish *you*, if you don't eat." Of course his sister laughed at this obvious rejoinder—laughed in the high, studied, infuriating whicker she'd picked up from her awful friend Mildred Creedy—but his mother laughed too, and that was hard to bear.

His father's face hung over the windowsill, shiny and clean above a fresh collar. How wonderful to be able to just get out of bed, climb into long pants, scrape soap off your face while you look at yourself in a mirror, eat a big breakfast, and then walk to work, where you sit down in your clean clothes and have interesting talks with other men.

"I'm sorry, Father, but I'm not through yet." That was the right tone: firm but not insolent. "I'll wait till I'm done."

"Oh, drop it, you little martyr, and come eat."

So Jemmy came in to sit, sullen and pained, by his sister, who was forking great folds of pancake into her face and generally acting like the pig she was. His father didn't look up, his mother was busy at the stove. Jemmy wouldn't have given a dime for the lot of them.

But then his mother set a tall stack of food in front of him, holding one hand in front of her forehead as though her pinned-back hair might come unmoored and cascade into the plate. At the same time his father said, "Give him a drop of coffee, Grace. He's been doing man's work this morning."

His mother poured an ounce of coffee from the big blistered pot that was twice as old as he was and set it down by his milk. He sipped at it—it tasted like dirt and burned his tongue—and said, "That's good." Then he felt light-headed and wanted to cry, he liked his folks so much. The weather was making him feel funny.

He steadied himself by sucking up his pancakes and asking for more. As he worked on the second pile, he began to see the weather was getting to his parents, too.

An ugly fan of red and white speckles ran up from his father's collar to just beneath his chin on the left side of his face, and his mother was being short with his sister.

When Edith asked the question she'd been pressing since late June—"How old are you, Mommy?"—his mother didn't laugh and say, "A lady never tells," the way she usually did. She glared over her shoulder with her arms raised to the cupboard and said, "I'm twenty-eight and I feel like I'm ninety every time you ask that."

"That's so old," piped Edith. Jemmy's mother forked a pancake onto her plate so fast it seemed she'd thrown it across the room. "Eat," she said, already back at the cupboard. "See if you don't think it's more fun than talking."

"Now, Grace—" his father began, but then he got a pancake too and, giving Jemmy a neutral wink, bent silently toward it.

Jemmy saw a chance to be virtuous in the face of his sister's infamy, and composed a nice sentence: I feel much stronger now,

Mother, and I'll finish the wood. But he held his tongue; parents could be uncanny about motives, and this was a morning when his mother was ready to root them out. Instead, he finished his breakfast while his father complained about going to work on a Saturday.

"They might as well give us no day or the whole day. Half a day is nothing, doesn't even feel like half a day. I'll be beat hollow by noon, a day like this, and what kind of a half day is it when you come home all played out?"

Jemmy's mother, hanging cups on their hooks with angry little clicks, said, "You come on home, John. I'll still be working."

"Oh, now, Grace." Jemmy's father winked at him again and Jemmy smiled and picked up his coffee cup, but didn't drink from it. "Course you work all the time. But when I get home we'll have some nice ice water. Doesn't that sound good? Nice glass of ice water. One for each of us, because it's Saturday. Maybe two, if you're up to it."

Grace clicked the cups on their hooks. They didn't own that many cups. She must just be rattling them.

"What about that, some ice water? Or"—his father gave Edith a wink, but Edith didn't see it because she was sulking over her empty plate—"or maybe I could get some cold beer in and perhaps you'd have just a little of it, as a specific. We could go up to our room where it's cool—"

"Why is it cool in your room?" Edith broke her sulk to ask.

"Well, your mother and I, we can make it cool up there, honey."

"How?"

"Why, the cold beer, of course. But you kids'll be off swimming, so you'll just have to take my word for it. You kids'll be out of the house."

"I may be in the house," Edith said.

"I doubt it," said Jemmy's father. "I very much doubt it."

Then Jemmy's mother turned from the cups and laughed. "John, you're terrible."

Jemmy's father gave him another bland wink, but Jemmy knew he'd been cut out of it. His father hadn't said anything worth laughing about and certainly hadn't said anything "terrible." His parents were talking in code again, the way they always did. He'd sure be out of the house that afternoon. He'd be with Billy Toback. With Billy, at least you knew what was going on.

But Billy was as mean and out of sorts as everyone else this day. After Jemmy's father dismissed him with a light swat on the rump—"Finish the wood this afternoon," he said—Jemmy had run over to Billy's house only to find his friend sullen, lackadaisical, and not a bit glad to see him.

"C'mon, Billy, let's go swim."

Billy, dawdling around the kitchen sucking on a piece of lump sugar, said, "What for?"

Before Jemmy could answer this very stupid question, Billy's father came through the kitchen, picked his lunch pail off the table, and started for the door.

"Howd'ja do, Mr. Toback?" Jemmy asked politely.

Mr. Toback kept on going and slammed the door behind him.

"Why's he always so mad at me?" Jemmy asked.

"Dunno," said Billy.

Actually, Jemmy knew. The winter before, Jemmy had asked his father why Mr. Toback never smiled at him. His father must have had a bad, long day because he gave Jemmy a real answer without even thinking about it. "He's mad at you, son, because I wear a suit to work. He runs a band saw and I work in the store, so it makes him mad."

"But that's not my fault." Jemmy had a child's direct sense of justice. If his father had taken Mr. Toback's suit and made him wear overalls, then there was reason for anger. If not, it didn't signify.

"Not mine either," his father said. "I don't even make more money than he does. That's mostly what gets people sore. But Toback just likes to get mad at things. He's got a wild hair up—" His father broke off and called, "Grace, there any coffee?"

"A wild hair up what? What's a wild hair?" But his father wouldn't answer any more questions.

The sight of Billy pouting into the dry sink nearly pulled that explanation out of Jemmy, but he thought twice and started to wheedle instead. Finally Billy gave a listless nod and they went out together into the acrid morning.

The men walking toward the mill looked isolated and insubstantial; the street steamed dust under Jemmy's feet.

"The air's like dirty water," he said to Billy.

When they got beyond the town, the tall grass held the smoke and it would have been like walking through a low autumn fog, except for the heat.

They got to the pool, shucked their clothes, and jumped in. "Hee-hoo," cried Jemmy, and splashed water on Billy. Billy splashed him back, but it was too warm and still and both boys felt sluggish and out of sorts. Jemmy floated belly up and said, "Good thing there's no girls to see." Billy didn't even smirk.

Jemmy, on his back, saw the sky divide itself into clouds, with veins of yellow light running down between the high bulges. "Lookit that," he shouted.

Billy looked up from where he'd been searching for a skipping stone, but the yellow was gone, the sky gray and close again.

"The sky looked funny," Jemmy said.

Billy gave a man-of-the-world shrug and returned to his search.

"It did," Jemmy insisted.

"Call me when there's a circus," Billy said.

Jemmy floated, thinking this was shaping up to be one of the most miserable days of his life.

"It did," he repeated feebly. Then he heard the noise.

"See," he said, "it's a funny day."

"See what?"

"Listen."

Billy listened, and heard it, and he and Jemmy climbed gravely out of the water and started putting on their clothes.

There was not a breath of wind, but all the bushes along the shore were rustling and clicking, and you could see the dry, pale underside of leaves, just as though a thunderstorm were on the way.

John Stockholm watched Jemmy scamper from the house and felt magnanimous.

Grace quit all her cup-rattling and said, "John, you know he should finish his chores before he goes out."

"I know, I know." Stockholm assumed a burlesque doleful look and saw his wife turn back to the cups to hide her smile. He felt lickerish—

usually did on Saturdays—the more so on a particularly foul day like this. "It's amazing, isn't it," he said to Grace's good back, "how sometimes the weather doesn't matter."

Grace brought a mug of coffee over to the table and sat down in the chair Jemmy had fled. "It may not matter to you, with your clean cuffs. But I'm putting up preserves today. Edith, go tidy up your room."

Edith looked up from the delicate figures she was etching on her empty plate with a fork tine. "Mommy, I'm eating."

"You're through eating. Go tidy your room."

Edith rose, quickly enough to turn away wrath, but slowly enough to show she understood the injustice of the order, and left the kitchen on heavy feet. She clomped upstairs for the better part of a minute.

"Some breakfast," said Stockholm.

Grace sipped her coffee. "When he gets home he'll have to stack the wood and then draw the bath water too. He's forgotten the bath water. It'll make him contrary."

Stockholm reached over and closed his hand lightly around her wrist. "Grace, everybody's contrary, a morning like this. We just have to weather it through. I'll bring back the beer, and the preserves can wait."

Grace glanced toward the stove, which was already swelling with its ability to turn a bad day ghastly.

"Think I can let it go a day, John? I don't like to do that."

"Sure. Wait until tomorrow. Then I can help you."

They'd been holding hands across the sticky table. She pulled hers away. "Does wedlock mean I have to take that with a straight face? When was the last time you helped me in the kitchen?"

He snatched her hand back, clapped it to his knee. "When was the last time you earned a dollar in the store?"

"I could have had old Amos Candage at the bank, and he'd earn his money and not make me take it out in preserves. We'd have somebody to do the preserves and somebody else to do the cooking."

"That's all true, but he couldn't give an afternoon like I'm going to."

"John, it's a bigger miracle than Easter that we have only two children."

Stockholm pushed himself up from the table and put on his go-to-work hat. "That's blasphemy, Grace. Be nice to me, or I'll tell your mother."

She kissed him. "Be careful how you treat me, John. With that hat, you'd stay a widower forever."

He was still perversely buoyant out on the choking street. Working half a day was bad, but it was better than a full day, and there was a broad, empty day after it, when he could buy the family ice cream and walk them around the town and everybody would think what a fine brood he had.

The street was nearly empty but he wouldn't be late. He ran the company store, and didn't have to be waiting at his post when the working day began. As he walked through the gate of the Brennan mill, the final whistle blew, all the donkey engines opened up, and the first log met the head-saw with a looping hell of noise.

You could hear that noise in your teeth, but it didn't bother Stockholm at all. He liked the bigness and the violence of the operation, and the complexity. To prepare for that hyena screech, filers had been working since dawn, scraping the gullet cracks out of the lethal blue length of the band saw. Then, strung taut around its ten-foot flywheel, the endless, supple steel blade would start moving its teeth at ten thousand feet a minute. Toback, a capable head sawyer for all his surliness, would signal with a thumb and index finger—there could be no talking heard above the din—to his setterman. Toback had the sheets from the mill superintendent, who'd probably want the day to start off with 6/4, six quarter inches, a one-and-a-half-inch cut. Clyne, the setterman, would get the log dogged down, and then ride the carriage along with it, right past the blade that sang murder inches away from his ear, and then gig back again for the next cut. And the long slices of lumber would fall away like cards off a deck, the bull chain would pull new logs up from the pond, the clanking friction nigger would slap them onto the carriage, and the setterman would ride again into a stinging froth of sawdust and sap. All day, tree trunks would race dripping into the saw to become planks—two hundred thousand board feet of them a day.

Stockholm, would sooner have earned his living as a shooting gallery target than ride the carriage, but he liked being part of a combine where men casually handled such awesome tools. And—he paused a moment, on the threshold of the store—he did like going to work in a suit. Maybe Toback had seen something of the dandy in his behavior. Well, it didn't matter a whole lot; he wasn't about to change his ways to please Toback. Stockholm's own father, a burly Norwegian river pig, had muscled logs into the Saginaw all his life, until he dropped dead on the job. He could have whipped two Tobacks, and he lived long enough to see his son take over the company store, and was happy to see it. Stockholm stood for a moment while the mill howled into life around him, thinking of his father tramping into the house with a crust of Copenhagen snuff on his chin.

Then he stepped inside the store, glanced around to make sure the stock had stayed tidy overnight, and said hello to his bookkeeper. The man's name was Peter Main, and Stockholm delighted in him. He had the shoulders of an ox, a pirate's face with one dead eye and black patch to cover it, a right hand so big his pen stuck out of it like a straw testing a pie, and the fussy concern of an old-maid schoolteacher. He looked up as Stockholm entered and, instead of letting loose some terrible oath from the Barbary Coast, said, "Good morning, Mr. Stockholm. I'm at my wits' end over these Ames people. They've sent me an invoice for two hundred new shovels and I make it a hundred eighty-nine by my count. I can't see paying for eleven shovels we didn't get."

Stockholm smiled, thought of sending Main east to the Ames office to demand the missing shovels. "It's all right," he said, "I'll draft them a letter first thing. They'll make good on the shovels."

"I hope so," said Main pettishly, and bent back to his accounts.

Main talked the way he looked: a low lumpy voice full of menace. Even after two years, Stockholm still half expected him to leap roaring from his desk one day, and plunder Hinckley.

"Excuse me, Mr. Stockholm," said Main before Stockholm was half through checking his supplies of kerosene, "but did you get a chance to do that letter yet?"

"I've been here about four minutes so far today, Mr. Main."

Main, with his fixed look of rage and bloodlust, said, "I beg your pardon, Mr. Stockholm. I wasn't trying to force you. I merely meant to say I'd be happy to do the fair copy."

"Oh no, I'll do that. Have to earn an honest living." Stockholm did his own letters unless he was terribly pressed, or unless they were unusually important, when Briggs, the typewriter in the treasurer's office, would transcribe them.

Stockholm had no idea where Main came from. He'd been sent over by the superintendent when Stockholm's first bookkeeper went back East to care for his invalid mother. A month or two after Main arrived, Stockholm heard a story about a legendary figure called Mad Peter, a bullwhacker who fled his job after settling an argument with the camp cook by biting through the man's throat. But every lumberman loved to tell horrible lies about tougher lumbermen, and Stockholm didn't credit any of them. Still, he never quite dared ask Main where he came from.

Stockholm was halfway through a delicately phrased letter to the Ames people when Main said, "Can I light the lamps, Mr. Stockholm?"

Main's desk, off in the corner, was dark; and so was Stockholm's, now that he thought of it. He walked to the window and saw the whole mill yard dim as a winter's dusk. "Come take a look at this," he said to Main.

The bookkeeper came over the window, glared through it, and said, almost in a whisper, "Looks like Peshtigo."

"Peshtigo? Were you there?" Stockholm had been eight years old when the Wisconsin forest fire snuffed out twelve hundred lives. The Chicago fire had broken out the same day and it got all the press. Only the older loggers still talked about Peshtigo.

"Yes, Mr Stockholm, I was. I was a lad then, employed in the Gearson camp. It came on something terrible, but it looked just like this in the morning before it started."

"What should we do?"

"Do?" Main's good eye swung around to Stockholm, oddly calm in the wreckage of his face. "It may just go away. It may just be a"—he paused—"a fretful thunderstorm or a—you know, with the sun—"

"Eclipse?"

"Eclipse."

"Well, I don't think it's an eclipse."

"Neither do I, Mr. Stockholm." Main turned back to the window, curled his lips out from his teeth, and looked ready to eat puppies.

"John," he said, "you'd best go home and look to your family."

That's the first time he's ever called me by my first name, thought Stockholm. And before he could think on the rest of Main's message, Briggs, the typewriter, was at the door, saying that a fire had started in the mill yard and the superintendent wanted the two of them to come and help put it out.

Scott Keegan didn't know whether the mill whistle or his own coughing woke him, but there he was, awake in his room with the whistle screaming while he coughed into his pillow fit to die. He was coughing because the room was full of smoke, so much that at first he thought the hotel was on fire. But then he looked out the window and saw that the whole world was full of smoke.

He finished coughing and considered trying to go back to sleep. It was a gamble. He might go back to sleep and wake up to find a couple of hours happily vanished; or he might twitch and think bad thoughts and put himself into a black mood that would last all day. The black mood seemed likelier, so he swung out of the narrow bed, went over to the basin, and splashed water on his face. A flicker of movement went across the edge of his vision like a bad thought, but he turned fast enough to see it was a mouse, scampering to safety behind his sample case. He ran his tongue over his teeth and wondered if the mouse had dropped a litter on his tongue while he slept.

Sometimes shaving cheered him, or at least made him feel ready to walk through the day. But he wanted to take a shave in Craid's barbershop before he started trying to sell there, so he had to let that go. He rubbed his chin; it was rough and greasy and he felt like a bum.

Clean shirt. There was only one left in his suitcase, but that was all right; he could get his clothes washed in St. Paul tomorrow. He buttoned his shirt, poked the stud through its hole, and hooked the collar onto it. If the ravaged, venereal mirror above the dresser could be trusted, the effect was very crisp, and he began to feel better.

The stud broke. The tiny bulb jumped off the end and Keegan's collar snapped open and tumbled lightly down his back to the floor. He looked at the washbasin, fought the impulse to hurl it through the window.

"Aha," he said aloud, just like somebody in a play. The day before yesterday, Duluth's appalling heat had driven him in off the street to stand under a clothier's ceiling fans. He'd stayed there so long he'd been embarrassed to leave without buying something, and a collar stud was the cheapest thing he could think of.

He'd been wearing the green suit when he bought it, so it should be in one of the pockets. He plunged his hand into the ghastly tangle of his suitcase and found the stud.

He put on the maroon tie with the gold thread in it, then lifted the mattress from the bed and pulled out his pants. It was a nasty wafer of a mattress but its weight had kept the crease. Keegan climbed into the pants feeling fussy and old-maidish. It was a delicate balance, being a drummer. If he let his clothes go to hell, people wouldn't trust him. If he dressed too smartly, they wouldn't trust him either. He hated the ritual of holding the mattress aloft with his shoulder every night while he arranged his trousers on the wire grid that covered the springs. In the better hotels the grid was small; in the poorer, very wide. This was a medium hotel, and the grid had stamped a series of rectangles about the size of playing cards into his pants. But they would shake themselves out, and by the time he got to the street, he'd look good enough to fool the rubes.

No, that was wrong. That was what came from a bad night's sleep. No drummer was good enough to get away with scorning the rubes. It was one thing to swap rube jokes with other drummers in the smoking car, but if you carried that attitude into the field, you went bust. A rube could spot a snob over the hill in a blizzard.

Keegan was ready to go out and sell by the time he finished buttoning his jacket: he was looking forward to talking with salt-of-the-earth small-town folk, but he wasn't overly anxious to make friends. Happy in the anticipation of a couple of hours of mercenary camaraderie—which was about as happy as he got these days—he picked up his cases and went down to the breakfast.

As he passed through the lobby, a fiercely chipper desk clerk cried, "Morning, Mr. Keegan!"

"Morning. How'd you know my name was Keegan?"

"Oh, I keep track. Part of the job." The clerk bobbed and beamed. His perfectly round face seemed much wider than his shoulders. He looked like the man on signs in cheap restaurants who announced that the first cup of coffee was free with the sandwich.

Pleased to have inspired so much joy with no effort on his part, Keegan said, "Good for you. Nice hotel you've got here, but I thought it was burning down over my head."

"Oh yes, you mean the smoke." The clerk got so grave that Keegan gave him a salesman's smile to cheer him up. He cheered up right away. "It happens every summer," he said, "smoke all over, but nothing ever comes of it."

"So I've heard," said Keegan, remembering the dark-haired girl he'd spoken with yesterday afternoon.

"First time in Hinckley for you, Mr. Keegan?" The clerk didn't wait for a reply, but hurried right on, "Bet it is. Well, it's a nifty town, but it does get smoky in the summer. Now, if you'd come here a month later, you'd see the prettiest place on earth. And good hunting, too."

Soon he'll start talking about lakes, thought Keegan. Everybody in Minnesota wants to talk about their goddamn lakes. But he was wrong. The clerk produced a newspaper, pushed it across the counter to Keegan, and pointed to a chart.

"See," he said, "it's not always like this. It's just a dry summer, all around. Driest ever. Look here. In July of ninety-two the humidity was sixty point five percent, and last month it was forty-eight. See?"

"I never blamed a town for its weather yet."

The clerk was smart enough to see Keegan wanted to break off the conversation. "Breakfast still being served," he said, and nodded his head toward the dining room. "Take the paper, look through it. Printed right up the street by Mr. Hay, and there's those who says it's better than the Duluth *Herald*."

"Better than the Duluth *Herald*?" Keegan asked in a subdued, wondering tone.

The clerk's smile turned into an irritated pout. "Yes, Mr. Keegan," he said firmly.

Never try funning a rube about his town. Here was a burg so small that the Elks and the Masons probably knew each other's secret rituals, but everyone in it clearly thought it was worth two of Chicago. Keegan couldn't understand that: he'd never given much of a damn for Averill Park. Maybe that was part of being a good salesman: not preferring one place to another. He was at home in every drummer's hotel—the thin towel, the jammed window, the soap hewn from living marble, the chair with one short leg by the door all gave him the same sense of continuity he supposed householders got from the iron box that held the kitchen matches and the scented souvenir pillow from Maine that had "I pine for you and balsam" stitched across it.

Keegan made amends to the clerk by thanking him elaborately for the paper and choosing a table in the dining room where the man could see him reading it with acceptable gravity.

One of the headlines said "Fires in the Northwest—Damage being done in the vicinity of Hinckley—Section men get to work to fight the flames—Hundreds of tons of hay destroyed."

The smoke might just be part of Hinckley summer, but Keegan guessed the farmers whose hundreds of tons of hay had been destroyed were pretty sore about it.

He ordered sausage and eggs, but as the waiter left the table he called him back and changed the sausage to lamb chops. No point in punishing yourself just because you're having a dry spell selling.

But when the chops came, he didn't enjoy them. Even though they were first-rate chops, they'd cost an extra dime, and trying to pull an extra dime's worth of pleasure out of them made his stomach close up. While he sawed off small pieces of meat and pretended to savor them, he leafed through the Hinckley *Enterprise*. Big doings. "The lumber is on the ground for J. Oman's new residence north of the Eastern Minnesota gravel pit. The home will be built far enough away from the pit that the southern prospect will not be marred. Contractor Mills will build the house."

A Mr. Wett had ordered an Iver Johnson revolver for his son; it had taken two months to arrive, and when the boy fired it, the trigger came loose. The advertisement for the revolver had appeared in

Harper's Weekly, a New York City publication, and the Enterprise made it clear that the Wetts had gotten no more than they deserved. After all, they could have purchased a perfectly good revolver at Mr. Grundig's hardware store.

That tart little account didn't augur well for a Chicago drummer. Keegan turned the page, started to read about a picnic, then closed the paper. This wasn't his town.

He finished his breakfast thinking that not one article in that paper mentioned the name of a street—people lived north of the gravel pit or across from the tobacconist, or else a family name was given and the reader was expected to know where they lived.

Keegan put down thirty-five cents for the breakfast, went to the front desk, and gave the paper back to the clerk. "You're right. It's a grand paper."

"Why, thank you, Mr. Keegan. We're pretty proud of it."

"No wonder. Say, is it all right with you if I leave my suitcase here? I'm leaving this afternoon, but I have some calls to make first."

"Of course, Mr. Keegan." The clerk, more than placated, ran out from behind his counter and grabbed the suitcase. "I'll put it right here and keep an eye on it."

Keegan waved his thanks and walked out through the hall—which was decorated by a painting so inept that he couldn't tell if it was of a deer or a bull—to the street, where he ran into the dark-haired girl he'd seen yesterday.

Even in the smoke, even under the hot grit that was flaking down from the sky, she looked marvelous. He dropped his sample cases, pulled off his hat, and called good morning.

She started. "I beg—oh."

"Keegan. I saved you from the bird attack yesterday."

"Oh, yes, Mr. Keegan. You're here selling medicine, aren't you?"

"Certainly not," said Keegan, annoyed. "It's not a wonderful season for me, but I hope I don't look like—"

"Barber supplies. I'm sorry."

"Medicine! Why, I'd settle down here before I'd sell medicine."

"Would that be so awful?"

It wasn't his day for placating rubes. "I'm sorry. I only meant I'm used to moving around."

"No, you didn't," she said coolly. "You meant that you'd rather live here than sell medicine, even though you think it's disgusting here."

"I'm told it's pretty in the fall," said Keegan helplessly.

She startled him by smiling; he'd thought it would take five minutes at least to recover from his gaffe. "That's safe," she said. "Can you imagine it being less pretty than this?"

He started his full salesman's grin but decided it wasn't time for the big guns. "Most of Chicago's less pretty than this."

"Chicago. I was there once." She rubbed her forehead with the back of her hand. "What a dirty day. I was in Chicago. Do you live there?"

"I used to," he said. Then, without thinking, he told the lie he'd sworn to himself never to tell: "I left when my wife died."

"Oh, but you're so young." She looked upset and sympathetic.

"I've gotten over it," he said quickly.

"Nonsense," she said. "What's that you have? A barber thing?"

"Say, that's worth your while. It's pretty as a jewel." He stooped down, unlatched the wooden case, and revealed the miniature Congress Chair. "I bring this around to show barbers our best chair. It's easier to carry than a real one—but not much. It's a heavy little—Look." He pumped the lever and the seat rose. "It works just like the full-size one." He stopped short of describing the quarter-sawn oak; this woman was an unlikely customer.

Nevertheless, he wouldn't have traded her response for a sale. She stooped down gracefully right there in the street and touched the lever. "It's perfect," she said. "I see why you'd be mad I thought you were selling medicine. Look at it. It's just an old barber's chair, but it's so—do you think everything would be interesting if it were smaller?"

He knew what she meant, but he couldn't think of an amusing answer. They crouched together in the street, watching fine soot settle like talc on the seat and headrest of the Kraut & Dohnal Congress Chair.

"Well," she said, rising, "that's as fine a thing as I've seen in a while. You must do very well with it."

Keegan buckled it back in its box. "Didn't do me much good yesterday. Though if I'd had my wits about me I could have used it to brain the bas—barber."

Betty gave him an honest-to-God grin. "Was the bas—barber Mr. Turgeon?"

"I don't know."

"Was he across from the drugstore?"

"Yes. The 'Twilight's Last Gleaming Pharmacy' or something like that."

"That's almost right." Betty laughed. "Anyway, that's Mr. Turgeon. He's famous for being a tartar."

"Well, I couldn't have been stupider with him. I insulted him and his store and then tried to sell to him. He kicked me right out. Threw a catalog at me. That never happened before." Keegan looked around at the sullen, smoke-bound buildings. "Maybe I *should* open shop here. My luck's gone, and that's what a salesman needs most of."

"I don't think your luck's gone," said Betty hesitantly. "You're probably just sad about what you told me. About your wife."

Keegan shook his head.

"No. It's true, you are. You're sad, and if people aren't buying from you it's because they don't know you're sad about your wife. They probably think you're sad about what you're selling, and so they get scared off."

"I'll have a button made up that says 'My Wife's Dead' and wear it on my lapel. Do wonders for business."

Betty started coughing; Keegan thought it was the smoke, then saw she was trying to stifle a laugh. She looked at him, one hand cupped over her mouth.

"I must be crazy to think that's funny," she said through the hand. "That's horrible. I have to go. Thank you for showing me the chair, Mr. Keenan."

"That's Keegan. And you're welcome. And you're no dope."

Betty gave him an ironic half-curtsy and started off down the street.

"What's your name?" Keegan called after her.

"Langdon. Betty Langdon, Mr. Keegan."

Keegan watched her walk away while explosions of dust roiled up around her from the street with every step she took.

"My wife's not dead," he said to her back. "She just ran away."

Betty turned. "Excuse me?"

"I said, it was good meeting you."

She nodded, Keegan turned on his heel, stepped out strongly, and bounced off the flank of a tethered horse that had apparently been standing in utter silence behind him all the time he was showing off. The horse made a low, amused, rumbling sound, and Keegan walked around it, not looking back for fear of confirming his near-certainty that Betty had seen this vaudeville turn.

Betty smiled when Keegan ran into the horse, and laughed out loud when he kept on going, stiff-backed, without so much as glancing her way.

I like him, she thought. That's one on Winton Reese. Pleased to have Winton so easily outcharmed by drummer, she headed for the St. Paul & Duluth depot and a talk with Tom Dunn which, she was dolefully confident, would contain few surprises.

Still, she liked going into the depot. It wasn't quite what a proper young lady should be doing, and her visits there added a fraudulent savor to her wispy, one-sided love affair.

The sounder was filling the bay with its dry snapping, and Tom was bent toward it, listening. As Betty came up behind him his hand went to the key and drummed out a brief message. He always told Betty he wasn't a particularly good telegrapher, but she thought him miraculously deft and never quite believed that whole sentences could be broken down so quickly into mere clicking.

"What's all the talking about, Tom? Something important happening?"

He swiveled around in his chair. "Betty!" As always, he seemed delighted to see her; as always, he got cautious almost immediately. "What brings you here?" She wondered briefly if she wouldn't have given up on him long ago if he didn't show real pleasure for a few seconds every time they met.

"I had some shopping to do for Mother and thought I'd stop in and say hello. Are you terribly busy?"

"Naw. The old chawbacon down at Pokegama is complaining up and down the line about the smoke. I just told him it was smoky here, too."

"Well, it is." Betty brushed her hair from her forehead with the back of her hand. She'd read in a *Harper's* story about a girl who did that, and men found it enticing. She did it a lot in front of Tom; irritated at herself, she shook her head so that the hair fell back where it had been before. "It's as murky out as I've ever seen it."

The sounder rattled.

"Pokegama again," Tom said. "Says the sky's all yellow."

Betty looked out through the bay window; it was gray as February. "No yellow here. Maybe the sun's coming through down there."

"Maybe." Tom worked the key, listened to the reply. "Pokegama says it doesn't look like sunlight."

"Don't you telegraphers ever talk about trains?"

"You ever met anybody who'd rather talk about trains than weather?"

Betty laughed. "Only you. And by the way, I thought"—she paused, but it was too late; she hated how she could never move smoothly into things—"that you were going to come by last night."

"Oh. Well, I was stuck at the key. Sam relieved me late. He gave me an excuse I wouldn't dream of telling you."

"You might have come by anyway. It was too hot to sleep. I was out on the porch."

Tom laughed as though she'd made a joke. Then he mumbled something.

"What?"

The sounder started again. Tom answered it. "Pokegama again. Says—"

"I don't care about Pokegama. What did you just say?"

"Oh, nothing. Just that I thought you might have been tired from your afternoon with Winton Reese."

Good. Hinckley's superb gossip system had justified her trust in it.

"Why, yes," she said demurely, "Winton asked me out riding. But wherever did you hear about it? If you saw us, why didn't you say hello?"

"I didn't see you. Winton told me."

"*Winton* told you?"

"Yes. He came in about six—"

"Why? Why did he come in?"

"Said he wanted to check the schedules. Then we fell to talking, and he said he'd gone out driving with you."

"What else?"

"Oh, not much." Tom looked at the silent sounder. "Just that he'd had a pretty good time."

"I see. And what did you say?"

Tom shook his head. "Nothing."

"I know what he said. And I know why he came in. What I don't know is why you let him say those things about me. Do you really think I'd have anything to do with that stuck-up"—the words "soup stick" came into her mind, but it wasn't harsh enough. She gave Tom a fierce, level glance and said, for the first time in her life, "that stuck-up bastard."

"That's a fine way to talk," said Tom.

"Well, it's a fine way for you to act. You should have hit him."

"Hit him?"

"Yes. He tried to take liberties with me."

She knew that sounded pretty feeble after her terrific epithet of a second ago; ridiculous, in fact. If she looked at Tom's bland, unhappy face for another second, she'd start to cry.

"You should have hit him." She ran out of the office.

Tom reached out an arm, as though the gesture could draw her back into the station. "Betty, he didn't say anything awful."

The sounder started then, and Pokegama told him the yellow light was gone, but that it had become hotter and smokier.

Tom grabbed the key and hammered back, "Keep me posted on everything every five seconds." But he realized he was so flustered that he'd garbled the message and his uncharacteristic asperity had gone unheard down the wire.

Tom Dunn's father was a religious man. He didn't talk scripture and he didn't do any obvious praying. He didn't call on the Lord in times of stress, except when Tom would drop a side of beef in the sawdust, and then it was, "Goddamnit, you're dropping the meat. Goddamn!" But he made Tom go to church every Sunday, and one Fourth of July the Dunns had no fireworks because Tom's father had given the summer profits to help buy stained-glass windows for the Hinckley Episcopal Church. The windows were widely advertised as coming from Italy, but Tom saw the crates off-loaded from the train and they had FOB NEW YORK CITY stenciled all over them. The windows looked fine, though, once they were in place—a blue-eyed Jesus smiling at the little children, a lamb sleeping beside a tiger—and Tom liked looking at them during the sermon. But he didn't like it as much as he would have liked setting off Roman candles.

It didn't make him mad, it just didn't mean much, sitting in church listening to how people should behave, singing songs too sweet-natured to be rousing about Christian armies, looking forward to the good big feed that would be better if you got it on Saturday. Christmas was nice, because it gave him some feeling of what all the other days in church were about; even so, church never took. He went—he wouldn't dream of not going—but God remained to him a slightly dowdy figure, a good man who was kinder and more important than the governor of the state, but nowhere near as interesting as the President.

When he was twelve or thirteen, Tom would wander around in the spring feeling juicy, and idly try to ascribe his feelings to God's eternal love of man, palpably displayed in the sticky green buds on the branches of trees still gaunt with winter. Mostly, though, Tom felt it no more than his due to be able to go barefoot outdoors.

His father never talked to him about church, but Tom sensed the man's disappointment that he didn't take it more seriously. Every now and again, Tom would get guilty and try. But each time he did, he'd hear the minister preach about the awful Day of Judgment when the graves would vomit forth their dead. And that struck him as vengeful nonsense, especially after he saw the small, white body of Annie Pearson fished out of Grindstone Creek. She was five years old and hadn't had much of a chance to prepare for the harrowing rigamarole of Judgment Day. Death, Tom thought, was smaller and meaner than most people made it.

Never having had much faith, Tom went through few agonies when he abandoned it altogether. One Sunday he was still fairly credulous about what the minister said; the next, he found sitting in the pew was just another chore, less arduous than his work in the store.

But his father, the big, harsh man who cut through red muscle with a cleaver, believed that nothing so unholy as railroad telegraphy should stand between a man's real work and his God. Tom marked that, and gradually developed a bland sort of substitute religion. He would be decent all his life. He might never be a first-rank telegrapher, but he could always be decent.

He never understood why this timorous, offhand faith intruded on his life with Betty. He knew she liked him better than the others. He could banter with her easily. He could borrow the postures of manhood from the careless men who ran the railroad, who daily took risks with tons of hot metal and then wandered out through the roundhouse talking casual smut.

He chaffed with Betty, and she laughed, and looked beautiful. She'd chatter back, and they'd have a fine time. And then they'd be on her porch, the evening's joking spent, and Betty tilting her face up toward his. Then her face was broad and closed, the eyes shut or open and angling off past his head. The open eyes scared him; the pale lids of the closed eyes scared him. He would back off with a joke, and sometimes she'd answer with a joke. Sometimes she'd move away, grave and angry.

Often, in his bed, he'd flatten out his hands and then curl his fingers slowly in until his hands remembered her breasts the way they had felt the morning after the wreck.

Late or soon, she was bound to go off with Clyde Bricklow, who could sing a song and tell a joke—somebody else's joke—and rummage in a girl's drawers with the best of them.

He wished he were a better telegrapher. He wished he could watch Clyde Bricklow die in convulsions beside a parlor piano at a party. Once in a great while, he even wished he were the town's best butcher. Mostly, he wished he had the sand to grab Betty's breasts just the way he had the one morning he wasn't even thinking about it, and lie down with her in the pine needles around the trunks of the tall trees north of Grindstone Creek.

The day would hang green and dim over them, and when they stopped joking they'd hear the wagons going by out on the post road, but nobody would be able to see them where they lay.

Stockholm was amazed you could work with barrels full of water and still get so thirsty. Briggs, the typewriter who had summoned him to the job, was slightly built and above five feet tall. Stockholm followed him out to the yard and at first thought nothing of Briggs's backing off and directing the transfer of the water barrels from the wagons to Stockholm's arms. Men on the wagon bed would handle the slopping barrels down to Stockholm while Briggs, his shirt still clean, said things like "Easy, easy there!" and "That's the ticket, John." Of course, other men were taking the barrels too, and Stockholm supposed Briggs had a word of encouragement for all of them. After the first few trips, he began to hate Briggs. Stockholm would take a barrel—"Gently there, John!"—and lurch off with it spilling bright crowns of water this way and that until he came to whichever pile of lumber needed attention. There were a couple of hundred neat stacks of planks, every one built up with plenty of air space to dry the wood. The wind, freighted with sparks from the eternally smoldering swamp, kept fluting through them, carrying seeds of fire to new stacks.

Stockholm got the hang of it. You couldn't just slosh the water in through the end of a pile. You had to find where the nest of fire was, heft the barrel up on top of it, and tilt it slowly so that water soaked down gently through the lumber. In thirty seconds or so there would be a satisfying hiss and a rank smell and you could dump the rest of the water and return for a new barrel.

And when you got it, the immaculate Briggs would tell you to be careful with its contents.

After an hour of this, Stockholm, going out with a full barrel, heard somebody call, "Right, it's all done!" at the very moment a sawyer, coming in with an empty, bumped against him. Stockholm's barrel danced for a good four seconds, then somersaulted in a cunning way that drenched him from the crotch down.

"John!" Briggs cried. "Careful with that water. We need every drop!"

"Hell, sorry," the sawyer said.

"S'all right." Stockholm made himself smile. "Somebody just said it's out. You think it's out?"

"Looks like."

Stockholm turned to Briggs. "You little tick, go back to your lady work. I could get you fired."

Briggs hanging on the tall slats of a stake wagon, looked sadly around the yard. Men were loading empty barrels on the wagons. All the fires were out.

"I'm sorry, Mr. Stockholm." Briggs said humbly. "I suppose I got a little carried away. I'm sorry."

He climbed down.

Stockholm gave him a delicate clap on the shoulder. "No offense"—he couldn't remember the typewriter's first name—"Briggs, you did just fine. Sorry I got short."

"No, no," the small man said vaguely, turning toward the building that contained his machine. "Well, I'll get back to work now."

"Me too," said Stockholm heartily, ashamed to have been the one to close down the single great hour of the poor mutt's life, "but I guess I'll look in on my family first. It still might come on ugly."

"Good idea, Mr. Stockholm," said Briggs. He had no family.

On the road, Stockholm passed a couple of wagons driving in with water in case the fires started up again. Stockholm spotted the riven face of one of the drivers; it was Peter Main. He waved.

Main reined in. "Hello, Mr. Stockholm. Had you working, did they?"

"Sure did. I'd've collapsed for certain if it weren't for Briggs' magnificent leadership."

Main laughed. "Better to have him talking than carrying, I suppose. Where you headed?"

"Thought I'd go home and look in on the family. I don't like this day."

"Me neither," said Main. A gust of wind picked up half the street and blew it between the two men. Main disappeared in the harsh brown fog, but Stockholm heard him saying,"Come on up. I'll take you there and leave off a couple of barrels of water. They won't be missed at the mill, and it might be well to have them on hand."

"Right," said Stockholm. "Thank you." He climbed onto the buckboard beside Main. The wind dropped, the dust settled some.

"I saw Craig," said Main as they rolled toward Stockholm's house; "said he'll be calling out the boys in a little while if it doesn't brighten up."

"He's probably the only man in town who's happy today. May get a chance to try out his new engine."

Main nodded. "Regular Christmas Day for Chief Craig. But if I was him I'd have 'em all out there right now. These things come on fast."

"Well, if we get anything like Peshtigo, there's not a hell of a lot he can do one way or the other, is there?"

"Peshtigo." Main shook his head. "I remember at the end of the day I was in a hotel dining room. Don't have any idea how I got there, but I thought I'd never eat again, and then somebody put down a plate of biscuits, I must have eaten a hundred. Threw 'em all up, though. Anyway, there was a logger named Harner there. Big, scary man."

Stockholm wondered at the creature who could strike Main as big and scary.

"Some poor woman was carrying on, saying her husband had gone off down the logging road that morning, and had Harner seen him, and did Harner think he was all right? Harner kept saying he hadn't seen him, but that he was sure he was all right. The woman kept asking him again and again, and all of a sudden he started to cry like a baby and said, 'Lady, that road's corduroyed with dead men for twenty miles. There's not a chance in hell your husband made it.' So she screamed and fainted and Harner couldn't stop crying and people kept coming in so burned you knew they wouldn't last another twenty minutes, and the hotel people kept setting out biscuits. It was a nice evening."

Stockholm couldn't think of much to say to that. A block from his house the wind came up again, blowing dust along the street wheel-high, so that they seemed to be riding a barge down a muddy river, the backs and heads of the horses swimming along before them. The sky was the color of ash; Stockholm thought it would swallow up his arm if he raised it.

"Here we are," Main said. "Need help with the barrels?"

"Just hand them down to me. I've carried about a thousand today—two more won't hurt. Thanks very much, Pete. I'm surely in your debt."

"See you back at the mill?"

"I'll be there in twenty minutes."

Stockholm carried the barrels across the blowing yard to the porch. When he went inside he found Grace in the kitchen. She looked as though she'd been crying, but she managed a smile and said "You forgot the beer."

Stockholm kissed her. "I brought two barrels of water instead. Not as much fun to drink, but it'll never make you fat."

"Look at you. Have you been in a fight?"

"Yep. Brennan himself came in and said, 'John, you've done a fine job running the store in my mill, and I'm raising your salary by a thousand dollars starting this minute.' And I said, 'You greedy son of a bitch, that's not enough by half,' and I went at him. We fought for an hour or so and then I killed him, and I'm afraid we'll have to move."

Grace laughed some, but not as much as Stockholm thought his spur-of-the-moment fancy deserved. "Let's move right now, then. This is the weirdest day I've ever seen."

"Ah." Stockholm ladled water out of the enamel basin on the sink and drank until he felt nauseated. "I was in the mill yard helping put out fires."

"Fires!"

"Just a few little ones in the lumber. But I brought back a couple of barrels of water, just in case some sparks set the grass on fire or something. I have to go back to the store, but I'll come home right away."

"John, don't go back. It's already after one. Stay here. I know I'm being silly, but this day scares me to death."

He patted her on the shoulder and she moved quickly away to show him that a patronizing gesture couldn't make up for his absence.

"Grace, I just have to lock up. I'll be right back. Where's Edith?"

Grace smiled. "She's in her room sulking. Doesn't quite remember what made her mad, but she knows it's something. She's just hot. She likes to sulk when she's hot, and I like to scare myself to death."

"Jemmy?"

"He's off somewhere. He'll come back if it gets any darker."

Stockholm pressed her back against the dry sink and gave her a solid kiss. "Bring back the beer," she said when he moved away.

"I sure will. We'll have a time. But it's awful hot. I'm a little worried we'll drown in our sweat if we try any fancy business today."

"Very delicate," said Grace. "You're just like a lover in Sir Walter Scott's stories."

"I could not love thee, dear, so much, loved I not doing the company store accounts more." Stockholm blew her a kiss and went outside.

The wind had died away entirely, but everything had been dusted with gray powder and the yard was as colorless as a photograph.

When Stockholm started up the street, the wind came back so strong that he couldn't keep his eyes open against it.

A little before two o'clock a cloud of scalding ash blew across Chief John Craig's cheek. He wiped his eyes and pulled the rope. The firehouse bell sounded out clear, a flat, bright noise in the murky day. Craig rang it a dozen times.

Noble Barrett got there first. "Afternoon, John," he said, "think you'll get a chance to play with your new toy today?"

"Wouldn't surprise me any. I hear there's already been fires in the mill yard, but they put them out."

"Did they? Goes to show we don't really need a fire department, after all."

"You going to wear that?" Barrett was still in his white pharmacist's jacket. "I don't know if I want one of my men looking like some kind of sissy bandmaster."

Barrett didn't answer. He was studying the new engine. "Too bad we didn't get a chance to try it out first."

"Nothing to it," said Craig. "Nice thing about steam, it does all the work for you." He opened the firebox, saw there were plenty of shavings under the kindling, and dropped in a match.

"You do that now?" asked Barrett.

"Sure. That way there's steam up by the time you need it."

The small bit of expertise seemed to reassure Barrett. "Good. Fine. Here's Murray. Hello, Tim, I beat you."

"Had a customer," said the stationer. "Somebody wanted four bottles of India ink in the worst way, made me take out the corks to show 'em it hadn't dried up. Can you imagine fretting about something like that on a day like this? Where's the others?"

"They'll be along," said Craig. "I guess most of them's busy making certain their homes are all right."

"Think it's going to come on bad, John?"

"Nothing we can't handle." Craig closed a valve on the stack.

"What's that you just did?" Barrett wanted to know.

"Variable exhaust valve. Lets steam out of the cylinder and regulates the draft. Have to keep it closed until there's pressure."

"Damn all. You sound like you've spent your whole life doing this."

"They showed me the ropes in St. Paul, when I went up in the spring to look it over. I wouldn't spend two thousand dollars of town money without knowing what I was buying."

"Aw, hell, John," said Murray, "you'd spend two thousand dollars of town money just to run this thing once."

Craig grinned. "She *is* a beaut." The engine started to tick and creak as it heated up. "Look, look at that," said Craig. "First sign of steam in less than two minutes!"

Barrett and Murray agreed it was a wonder, and the rest of the men arrived.

"Come on, boys," said Craig. "Let's go put out a fire."

The men grabbed the pole and pulled the engine out into the street. Craig mounted his horse. It was blowing half a gale, hard and steady from the south, and the thin plume of smoke that had begun to rise from the stack disappeared. Pebbles, driven through the air at shoulder height, rattled off the boiler.

"It's worst to the west," called Craig. "Make for the west side of town, near the mill yard." The men started to trot up the street. "How much does this damned thing weigh?" asked Barrett, out of breath after the first fifty yards.

"Twenty-five hundred pounds," said Craig from his saddle.

"Less than a dollar a pound," Murray said. "Quite a little bargain."

"Nice to be sitting down, John?" Barrett's shoulders were getting sore.

"Save your breath, Noble. When you're fire chief you can ride to work too." Craig reined in, fell back, and rode along beside the engine, smiling down at it. This was a fine moment, going out with the new engine. He wouldn't have changed a thing, except the streets were empty; it would never have been nice to have some people on hand to cheer.

He got his cheers as the engine bounced heavily over the St. Paul & Duluth tracks. Two wagons, loaded with barrels of water and headed for the mill yard, stopped to let the firemen pass, and the drivers waved their hats. One of them shouted, "That's the ticket, Chief!"

Craig gave them a benign salute and Barrett muttered, "Hail, Caesar."

"Let's set up shop here," said Craig when they got to a clearing just beyond the mill, where fifty yards of parched hillside ran down to woods standing black and thick under the heavy pewter sky.

Craig had Murray and John Peterson, the butcher, run hose back to Grindstone Creek while he checked the gauges. As soon as he'd satisfied himself that he had forty pounds of steam—and that raised in less than ten minutes, what an engine!—Father Lawler came panting up. "Sorry I'm late, John. When I got to the firehouse, you'd already left."

Lawler, the town's Catholic priest, kept himself well liked by minding his own business. He wore his Popish vestments only on Sundays and he never told anybody how to behave. He didn't turn green around a little rough talk, and he could throw a mean, lolling curve ball that was the despair of the Pine City and Pokegama baseball teams. He loved the fire department and he kept his beads and other foreign kickshaws to himself.

"Afternoon, Father"—it was a measure of the man's popularity that Craig could call him "Father" without thinking much about it one way or the other—"don't worry. You haven't missed a thing. Don't she look grand?"

The two men admired the engine until Murray and Peterson returned.

"She's dunked," said Peterson.

"Good. Noble, John, grab that nozzle. Let's find out if we bought a pig in a poke."

Barrett and Peterson both lifted the hose, got into steadfast positions, and pointed the nozzle at the woods.

"Ready," said Craig. He nodded to Father Lawler. "Start stoking, but keep an eye on the firebox. Get her too hot and we'll burn the wheels." He twisted the try cocks; water jetted out. "All right, let's—Jesus, I nearly forgot to take her off her springs." He anchored the engine fast to the axles, then checked everything again just to be on the safe side. Good thing, too, because he'd forgotten about the exhaust valve. He opened the discharge gate and drain cock and took hold of the throttle. "Now"—was there enough oil on the link block? The hell with it—"here we go!"

Craig inched the throttle back; the engine started a sweet, greased chunking, barely audible over the wind. Everyone looked back down the length of hose and saw water come bulging through it toward them, moving with the swift deliberation of a cloud shadow. "Steady," said Craig quietly. "Hold her when it gets here." The hose stiffened in Barrett's hands, lifted right off the ground, and jumped out of Peterson's grasp. Barrett clung fast to the brass nozzle as a thick rope of water came creaming out.

"Damn!" yelled Craig.

"Got it now," said Peterson.

The two men leveled the hose and the water went into the woods in a hard white arc. The wind bent the stream to the right just before it disappeared into the trees.

"Damn, damn." Craig slapped the steam dome, burned his hand, stuck his fingers in his mouth. Barrett and Peterson held the hose, moved it back and forth; it was stiff as a drainpipe.

"Look at that!" Craig wiped his burned hand on his pants. "Two hundred feet if it's an inch!"

Everybody cheered until Craig closed the throttle.

"Well, boys," the chief said, his face bizarre as he tried to fight down a grin, "looks like we've got a good engine here. Let's get some oil on her."

As they slapped best-quality lard oil on the valves, the wind dropped away.

"Maybe there'll be nothing to use her on," Barrett said.

"I don't know about that," said Father Lawler. "You ever see a day like this before?"

"Those woods look ugly," said Craig. In fact, he thought the woods looked terrifying. He couldn't see anything burning, but the forest seemed to be feeding darkness up into the darkening sky. Every so often a sourceless light would show the sawtooth edges of the pines nearest the clearing.

"We'll just have to wait and see," said Craig. He looked over his shoulder. "They seem to have things under control in the mill yard."

They waited. Barrett lay down on his back, then lifted himself on one elbow in a picnic pose. Craig's horse nuzzled the dry ground. The wind started up again, blowing from the west this time.

"What's that?" said Murray.

"Wind," said Barrett.

"No, that noise in the woods."

They listened and heard a dull, distant thumping as though heavy things were being knocked over, far away.

Murray tugged at his crotch. "Hot. Sounds like something in the woods."

"Pretty smart of you," said Barrett, "to guess right away it was coming from the woods."

Murray looked down at him. "You must be being snotty, Noble. Because you're sure not being very funny."

"And you must be being stupid, because you're sure not being very smart."

"Stop it," said Craig.

"Well, I don't want some greasy fizzle of a pill pusher making mock of me."

"And I don't want you telling me how to behave, Craig." Barrett stood up. "You may be fire chief, but you're not my father."

"Are you absolutely sure about that, Noble?" Murray asked in a polite, interested way.

"Now listen, I'm not interested in hearing a lot of horseshit—"

"Shut it down, Noble," said Craig, "there's children here."

Jemmy Stockholm and one of Toback's boys had appeared during the squabble and were examining the engine.

"Hello, boys," said Barrett sullenly.

"Hello, Mr. Barrett," they chirped in unison.

The woods gave forth a low, grating rumble. Deep inside them, Craig saw brief glimmers of light, dirty orange like embers in the back of a coal stove. The wind was carrying pebbles again; the fire engine chimed as they hit it. The sky was right down on top of the trees.

"Boys," said Craig, "you'd best run along to your homes."

Jemmy Stockholm looked desolate. "We want to see the engine, Mr. Craig."

"No. You run along."

"Why?" the Toback boy boldly demanded.

"Because," said Craig, "in just a little while it's going to be hell with the door open around here."

The boys headed back toward the mill yard. The wind rose and fell, rose and fell. Barrett and Murray began picking at each other again, and Craig shut them up. The other volunteers were restless, too. Sim Olafson, the baker, kept dropping spit between his shoes and Peterson was whittling a stick, swearing as each cut went wrong.

"The fire going to come soon?" asked Father Lawler.

"I don't know. I think so." Ever since he'd shut down the engine Craig had had the feeling, familiar but unsettling, that this had all happened to him before: the waiting; the idle, nervous men; the machinery ready to be used.

Murray started to tell Peterson about the customer wanting him to check the India ink bottles. Barrett broke in to say that that story was boring the first time he heard it, and intolerable twice.

Craig told everybody to keep still and watch the woods. The

woods rumbled and glowed. Craig went over to the engine and checked the gauges, teased all the while by the feeling that he'd made these same rounds before.

The hole in his cheek gave a twinge. That was rare these days. Then it came to him. He didn't think back on the war much because he hadn't liked a single thing about it. But—he tongued his old wound—here he was, Sergeant John Craig, Company D, Third Minnesota Volunteers, stuck up on Culp's Hill during the second day of Gettysburg, trying to keep his men quiet through the long, simmering afternoon. He'd walked up and down the line with the skin on his face jumping until he was sure the boys could see it, telling them to lie easy, they'd be coming soon. Keeping them all resting on their rifles waiting for the attack that hadn't begun until the first stars were out.

Craig turned away from the nervous, eager firemen and spat through his cheek. I'm too old for this, he thought.

Ed Barry, at the throttle of engine 105, pulled the Eastern Minnesota southbound freight into Hinckley at 2:45 with his eyes running and his mouth sandy. The smoke had gotten so thick he'd had to light the head lamp back in Sandstone.

As they drew into Hinckley, Alex Thistle, Barry's fireman, looked back out of the cab and said, "Jesus, Ed, I can't see more'n half the train. I'm glad this run's over." Their job was to take freight cars down from Duluth, drop them off in Hinckley, then pick up northbound freight and head back the way they'd come.

Barry coughed against the back of his glove. "Looks like Voge got their new fire engine to 'em just about in time."

"Wonder if they've had a chance to learn how to run it since yesterday?"

"I can't think of a better time to learn."

"It didn't look like a whole lot of fire engine for the job."

"I ain't seen any fire yet."

"Naw? Figure this smoke is from folks cooking lunch?"

As Thistle spoke, a tool shed forty feet away exploded into flames. Nothing was burning near it; it just went up. The door fell away from the hinges, and for a moment the trainmen saw the contents—half a dozen lanterns, a pick, two shovels, a claw bar, and an inexplicable feather duster—looking oddly gay and inviting in the fierce light.

"God almighty," said Barry, "you see that? Let's unhook the drag and get the hell out of here."

He ran engine 105 down to the south end of the yard.

"Where is everybody?" Thistle wanted to know. "I don't see a soul stirring."

Barry put on the air and stopped the train.

"Probably out fighting the fires."

"They'll have fires of their own right here in a minute."

William Campbell, the conductor, pulled himself up onto the deck.

"What do you make of it, Ed?"

"Nothing good. There, look at it!" Barry pointed across the yard to a string of freight cars. A piece of burning debris sailed out of the woods trailing sparks and settled gently on top of one of them. For a moment the brand seemed to have died, but then a low, fat, healthy flame grew from the roof of the car and the wind pushed it along the whole string.

"We dumping these boxcars, Bill?" Barry asked. "I want to get shut of this place."

"We're dumping them," said Campbell, "but we can't go anywhere until the varnish comes in."

Barry remembered the southbound passenger train right behind them; they couldn't head back for home until it was out of the way. He spat black spit out his window. "Should be in now, shouldn't it? Who's the driver?"

"That'd be Bill Best."

"Best's a good runner. What's he doing laid out?"

"He's only late by a couple of minutes. He'll be here." The conductor jumped to the ground. "We're unhitched now. Let's coal up and turn her around."

Barry whistled twice and opened the throttle, and they started toward the turntable. Thistle grabbed his arm. "Ed, wait a minute!" Barry yanked the brake handle.

The roundhouse lay before them, vague as a fogbank in the dark afternoon, but before it the turntable showed clear, with every tie afire.

"Aw. Aw, hell," said Barry quietly. He was just twenty-one years old, and this was the first time in his life he hadn't wanted to be a locomotive engineer.

"What we gonna do?" asked Thistle.

As more ties took fire, a whole section of track lit up, an elegant S curve glowing brightly and evilly, bending off into darkness. Barry had a quick, idiot memory of a print that had hung in his grandfather's room when he was a child. It showed the Drunkards' Express, a locomotive with a skull for a cab, stoked by demons and pulling a carousing load of harlots and ginsucks over just such a track, through just such darkness.

Campbell climbed back into the cab. "You can't turn her around. Let's get up to the north end of the yard and wait for Best."

Charles Freeman, the brakeman, ran up to the cab waving an order book. "Bill!" Campbell looked down at him. "I got the numbers on the loads we have to bring back. Comes to thirty-five cars. But I don't see how we're going to make up the train."

An ember the size of a baseball tumbled from the sky and knocked the order book from Freeman's hand. He grabbed for it, but the wind took it and sent it flapping over the ground toward the burning freight cars. Freeman started after it. Campbell called him back. "Don't be a fool, Charley. We're not going to be making up any train today."

"But I got to have that book!"

"Leave it be. It's gone."

"Bill, the brasshats'll be all over me if I show up without it. I could get in real trouble."

The yard lightened a little as the roof of the roundhouse went up and a boxcar collapsed in a glittering spray of sparks.

"Real trouble, huh?" said the conductor. "Get aboard, you silly bastard. Ed, take her back."

Barry backed away from the roundhouse.

"You forgot to whistle," said Campbell; "you'll be in real trouble too." He laughed and shook his head. " 'Real trouble.' "

Barry backed to the depot, went in on the side track, and closed the throttle.

"Now what, Bill?"

"Now we wait," said Campbell.

The engine ticked and spluttered. The sky darkened until the world was black as midnight except where the yards burned. The wind was strong enough now to stir the coal in the tender.

"What's that noise?" Thistle asked.

"I just hear wind," said Barry.

"No. Listen. You hear it, Bill?"

Campbell shook his head.

"It's like a—I don't know—a waterfall, way far off."

Barry listened, heard nothing but the huge malevolence of the wind, and checked the gauges. "Where the hell's Best?" he asked and felt his voice break.

Campbell snapped open his watch. "He'll be along right away, Ed. Right away."

The fire killed the jacks first. It came booming up through the woods southwest of town and dropped the lumbermen with their axes still in their hands.

Dustin Emmons was sweeping out the kitchen in Brennan camp nine while Dan Chite, the cookee, opened cans for dinner with no idea that the men he was getting ready to feed were already dead.

All he knew was his kitchen was godalmighty dirty, getting dirtier, and old Emmons was making a damn poor job of cleaning it up.

"What's the matter with you, Emmons?" he asked.

Emmons dropped his broom. Chite was a pissant—all camp cooks were pissants, they got paid more than the jacks and fussed all the time anyway—and Emmons would have liked to see the little bastard try to last five minutes on a drive in the old days.

"You know what the matter is, Dan," he said pleasantly, for it didn't do for a bull cook to offend a cookee, "this wind is blowing all the crap in creation in here, and there's not a thing I can do about it."

"You could sweep a little faster," Chite suggested.

That was too much for a Saginaw man to take, even from a good camp cook. "I could, and you could open your cans of corned beef a little faster, and then everybody could eat for three days while you caught up on your sleep. Just open those cans, leave 'em out for the jacks, and work no hours a day instead of four."

"I work *hard!*" Chite squealed.

"You sure do dish out those dried prunes."

"They *like* dried prunes."

"You bet they do. But every now and again they might like a drop cake or some hot meat, too." Emmons paused for effect, then added, "The way Roothouse LaCourse makes it over at four."

Chite, in a moment of self-pity, had once complained to Emmons that LaCourse, the best cook the Brennan company had, got four dollars a month more than Chite did. Jacks liked to work where the best cooks were; the best cooks drew the best jacks.

"LaCourse!" Chite slammed the can he was hacking open down on the table. "Ain't a man in the camp thinks he's a better cook than me."

"No?" Emmons smiled. "Must've been mistaken, then. 'Scuse me."

"And you can bet your wrinkly old ass that LaCourse has a better bull cook than I do!"

"Prob'ly does," said Emmons mildly. He pointed to the half-opened gallon can of corned beef. "What's that you're cooking, Dan? Smells good."

"You know damn well we can't keep fresh meat in the—"

The kitchen bloomed white light. The western wall disappeared. Emmons didn't even have time to get scared. He saw Chite's mouth shut down and Chite's eyes get big. He saw the point of each serration on the top of the corned beef can blaze blue-white, sharp and tender; saw the black plank of shadow the can put across the table behind it; and saw the potatoes in the basket by the stove with all their wens and bulges, and the dirt still sticking to them. Each granule of dirt so clear.

The fire pounded and billowed through the forest, burning the trees, burning their roots in the ground, burning the topsoil and leaving incandescent clay behind. It fed itself on the air, burned through the sky eating oxygen, threw itself this way and that as it met invisible rips and flaws high in the ether.

It rolled over the outlying farms with huge, dumb prankishness: it sent a narrow red column down from the sky to consume a baby in its flour-barrel cradle, but left the grass standing in the field around the infant; it melted a metal plow but left the paint on a wooden one a few feet away.

A single thread of flame trickled into the kitchen window of Karin Hjerpa's farmhouse and set her hair on fire. In a quick, bad decision he would remember every hour of his life until his mind broke under the weight of it, her husband, Nels, grabbed a bucket from the floor and doused her. The bucket held kerosene.

Pulling darkness along with it, the fire took the small farmsteads and came on toward Hinckley, where the streets were made of sawdust and the buildings of wood.

"That noise," Barrett shouted over the wind, "it's like a waterfall. What is it?"

Craig squinted at the turbulent woods and at the tall black cloud above them. "That's the fire coming, Noble."

"Can we hold it?"

"Sure we can hold it." But Craig thought his pretty new engine looked feeble, almost frivolous when you listened to what was going on in the forest.

The wind rose, blew the smoke back from the stack of the fire engine in a flat, steady stream. A big piece of debris—a God-honest log—lifted out of the forest and, burning, tumbled over and over with a terrible comical slowness, right out of the woods and onto the hillside a hundred feet away. Craig opened the throttle. "Hit that, boys."

Peterson and Barrett leveled the bucking hose at the log, doused it, and actually sent it rolling back a few yards. Craig closed the throttle and everyone cheered.

"Save that for later," said Craig. "There's a lot more like that one still left in the forest." Nobody heard him.

Murray said something.

"What?" Craig yelled.

"The cloud. What's happening to the cloud?"

The smoke that had hung over the woods round and clearly

defined as a pile of black pillows was gone. So, too, was the last of the daylight.

"We're in it now," Craig said. "It's moved over us." He could make out the faces only of the men closest to him. "I'm opening her up."

"What should we hit?" somebody asked.

"Doesn't matter. Just wet down the ground in front of us. But I want the water there when we need it."

He walked to the engine—he could see the froth of sparks streaming from the stack—and opened her up. Water surged from the hose, arced away into darkness. "I wish we had a bigger engine," said Murray. "This is like trying to stop it with a music box."

"Pack it away," said Craig; "nothing's happened yet. The engine's plenty big enough."

A great fan of gray-yellow light opened up from the woods; the trees in front of it snapped back and forth like buggy whips.

"Is that the sun coming out?" Murray asked hopefully.

"Naw," Craig said, "it's the Holy Ghost come to help us." He looked around to make sure Father Lawler hadn't heard, and saw the priest in shouted conversation with a teamster who had brought a wagon of water barrels from the mill. The barrels were open; the water reflected the light, a dozen cold yellow circles.

Father Lawler trotted up the hill. "Good news, Chief. They're coming from the mill to help."

"What about the mill?"

"They've got a man on the whistle there. He'll sing out if it takes fire."

"Good. Go on back and tell them not to run over my hose."

The light warned a little, brightened, and then disappeared. A ball of black-red, dirty flame rose from the forest like a balloon and drifted toward the firemen. It passed over their heads fifty feet up and exploded into a shower of sparks.

Murray grabbed Craig's arm. "What the hell was that, Chief?"

"Never saw anything like it. Come on, get that hose around and put out those sparks!"

Barrett and Peterson hosed down the hill behind the engine and got most of the sparks; the mill hands took care of the rest.

"That was easy," said Barrett.

"Christ, look now!" Peterson shouted.

Five, six—a dozen fireballs sailed from the woods, crossed the dark sky like comets. The mill whistle began to blow, thin and distant under the hollow tumult of the wind.

In the carnival glare of the burning freight yard, Barry and Thistle fretted and swore. A steady torrent of sparks flowed through Number 105's cab, and engineer and fireman swatted at their necks as though trying to drive away blackflies.

"Son of a bitch! Where's Best? The town'll go in a minute." Thistle tried to spit on the deck but his mouth was too dry.

"And where'd Campbell get to? I want orders, is what I want." Barry was able to control his fear enough to keep it down to a level of grating petulance.

Neither man much wanted to look into the yard; they kept staring at the gauges, which were hard to see, even with the cab light going.

There was a great metallic flapping noise, as though steel curtains were being shaken just outside the cab; the wind was picking up ballast and flinging it against the locomotive.

"How about just taking her out?" shouted Thistle. "How about that?"

"I can't do that, Alex. You know I can't. I got no orders."

"What if Campbell's dead? I bet he's dead."

"Nobody's dead. He only left a second ago."

"You don't know. Where's Best? Where is he?"

More freight cars took fire and briefly lit up the empty track in front of the depot. Thistle tugged at Barry's sleeve. "He ain't coming! I bet the bridges are all out."

Darkness came down again, but a minute later, when a dull yellow light cut through the smoke, there on the main track was engine Number 125, a sooty, panting 4-4-0, the single most beautiful sight Barry had ever seen.

"Goddamn!" he yelled. "Goddamn, Alex."

"Well, look at that," Thistle said quietly.

Best swung down from his cab and ran toward them as the yellow light left the sky.

" 'Lo, Ed," he said, climbing into the cab, "had quite a time getting here."

"Didn't even see you come in, Bill. You ain't going to try to get through to St. Paul?"

"I damn near didn't get this far. I'm going to back out."

"Luck to you, and thanks for clearing me." Barry tugged the whistle cord and reached for the throttle. Best took hold of his wrist. "Leave it a minute, Ed. We'll be taking people out with us."

"I don't see anybody wants to go."

"They'll be coming. This town hasn't got ten minutes."

"Aw, hell, Bill." Barry heard himself whining, didn't care. "The ties are all burning. The rails'll spread and we'll all be stuck—"

"I'm senior here," Best said in a conversational tone, close to Barry's ear.

"And I've got right-of-way."

"You just wait, Ed. It'll be fine. Where's your conductor?"

Barry shook his head, breathing hard against tears.

"Hold still till I find him."

Best scrambled down to the smoking ground. Obscure fires showed here and there in the murk, but they gave no real light. The world swam in a black, choking haze, with the cab of Barry's engine floating overhead like a haven—a dubious haven, what with the streaked, terrified face Barry was poking out of it. Best gave what he hoped was a cheery wave and set off down the train to find the conductor. He'd been driving since before Barry was born, but he'd never seen a day like this. He tripped on something, recovered, and saw a lantern bobbing his way.

"Where's the freight conductor?" he called to the lantern.

"Here. Campbell. Who's that?"

"Best, with the southbound passenger."

"Hoo-ray!"

Best grinned and the two men met over Campbell's lantern in a pocket of stained light.

"Come with me," said Best, "I want you to talk with my conductor."

"Who's that?"

"Hiram Powers."

"Good. He's senior to me, and welcome to it."

They picked their way across to the passenger train. "Hiram!" Best shouted.

"Here!" Powers yelled from six feet away.

"We better hook the trains together," Best said, "pick up some folks, and get out of here."

Campbell lifted his lantern, nodded to Powers. "You'll be backing out. The turntable's gone."

"That's all right," said Powers in a startling Yankee voice, nasal, grating, and canny, "but we'll need to be taking on water. The track open?"

"Switch is open, but I don't know if the track's still there."

"Don't make no nevermind. We've got to try—can't go another five miles, we don't get water."

"I'll tell Barry he's got to wait," said Campbell.

"Tell him gentle," Best said, "he's getting itchy."

A stream of sparks spilled straight down from somewhere overhead.

"Don't blame him any," said Powers. "Hold fast, and we'll come back and pick you up."

Best climbed into his cab, which most of the time was a fine place to be. He'd spent his money to nickel-plate the throttle and reverse and put burgundy plush cushions on the seat boxes, and had hung up a tin lithograph of a big-breasted girl in gauzy robes who was kissing some kind of leaf and was cryptically identified as "The Spirit of Oregon." His fireman, George Ford, said it was like driving a whorehouse, but Best knew Ford liked running with him.

"We got to jerk soup," said Best.

Ford nodded. " 'We,' huh?"

Best whistled, opened the throttle, moved forward blind. The road felt spongy underneath, but the rails held. "We're going to hook onto the freight train and pull out all the people we can."

"All right." Ford wasn't much of a talker.

Best was creeping forward by guesswork—just drooling a little steam in every now and then; he'd never driven slower—when something took fire nearby and showed the water tank standing black on its skinny legs.

Best closed the throttle.

"Nearly ran by her. Think you can do it, George?"

"Yes."

Best watched as Ford climbed on the tender and tugged at the manhole cover. He wrenched it this way and that until a gust of sparks sent him staggering back into the cab.

"She's stuck," he said.

"Jesus, George. Is there—"

"I'll unstick her." The fireman returned to the cover, prized it open, and then reached up and pulled down the water spout. You always took a bath watering up at Hinckley; the spout was hung too high. Still, Ford made pretty good work of it until a wind-driven barrage of what seemed to be burning chunks of coal forced him to the cab again.

"We got enough, George?"

"Nope."

Ford went back out. The spout had snapped up as soon as he'd let it go, and he had trouble fishing it back down. Best heard a shrill noise through the steady pummeling of the wind and realized he'd been holding the whistle cord in his anxiety.

As soon as Ford got the spout down, a fat blade of flame came out of the darkness and touched his hands. He went back to the cab.

"Not sure I can do it."

Best reached for the throttle. "We got some, anyway—"

"Wait."

On his third try, Ford got the nozzle almost on top of the manhole, and the water ran fast into the tank. Sparks came streaming at him, first from the west, then from the south. Leaning on the spout, he swung this way and that, trying to keep his back to the embers. Best saw one hit him in the eye. Still Ford hung on until the water sloshed over the rim of the manhole. He started for the cab, turned, slammed down the cover, then tumbled in beside Best, his face puffy and bleeding. "Let's head for the barn," he said.

The moment he entered Albert Craid's barbershop, Keegan's day became glorious.

As he opened the door, he glanced up at the light fixtures because they were lit, and saw that they were two-light 200-candlepower models, oxidized copper finish, with a two-quart capacity and thirty-inch spread. Kraut & Dohnal was the only company that sold those particular lamps.

Pleased out of all proportion by this discovery—he was still rankling from his run-in with Turgeon and that barber's savage allegiance to the Koken company's products—Keegan set down his miniature chair and advanced beaming on the barber who manned the shop's single chair. It wasn't a Kraut & Dohnal chair, but the cabinet sterilizer was, as were the half dozen waiting chairs, which were filled with Hinckleyites in various degrees of beardedness. They were talking together, and two or three looked up and nodded as he came in.

The barber, a bald man in a soiled white jacket left his charge lying back with lather on his face and came smiling over to meet Keegan.

"Morning," he said, and stuck out his hand. "I'm Albert Craid."

"Morning. Scott Keegan."

"Stranger here, aren't you?"

Keegan nodded, thought of a couple of ploys, dropped them, and said, "I'm just in for the day. I'm a drummer for Kraut and Dohnal."

Craid's eyes widened. "No!" He turned to the men in the chairs. "Boys, wasn't I just saying how I needed a lot of new stuff, but how I was too busy to get around to ordering it?" The boys nodded and one said, "This mean I'll be getting my mug, Al? You've been promising it for just about a year now."

"Aw, not that long." Craig laughed. "I guess so. Mr. Keegan, can you arrange for mugs?"

"Indeed I can," said Keegan softly, half afraid that any big show of enthusiasm on his part would make this shop dissolve like a dream, leaving him facing Turgeon again. "I can certainly arrange for a very attractive mug. And anything else you might need."

"Oh, I need plenty," Craid said.

"Plenty," said Keegan, almost whispering. Nothing like this had ever happened to him before.

"Well, to start with, I want a couple of chairs. The boys is taking such poor care of themselves these days, and getting so dirty and hairy—" The men along the wall snorted, and the one who'd complained about his mug said, "Don't get it too prettied up, Al, or we'll all go over to Turgeon." Craid winked at Keegan. "You see how long old Turgeon'd put up with your deplorable personal habits, Charley." Charley allowed as how Turgeon was pretty sour, but he still wanted his mug damn soon.

"Anyway, Mr. Keegan, I was saying that the boys is coming in so often in need of tidying up, I'll be taking on some help, so I'll be needing more chairs. I'm also thinking of a good-sized towel steamer—you have one of those?"

Keegan nodded, fighting the impulse to embrace Craid.

"Though I don't know if I ought to put a hot towel on Charley's face. I suspect the dirt is all that's holding it together."

Even Charley thought that was funny and everybody laughed. Keegan, an accomplished laugher, carried on and slapped his knee for an appropriate amount of time.

"And," his newfound benefactor went on, "I think I might spring for a mirror case. Just oak, though, 'cause I can't afford marble."

Keegan shook his head to indicate he considered marble gaudy, vulgar, and meretricious.

"I guess that's about all the big stuff. But I need a lot of odds and ends. Mugs for some of the boys, and soap and razors and so forth, things I'd like coming in regular. And Turgeon has these little rubber things with bumps on them he puts along a shelf and it keeps the bottles from sliding off. I don't know what they're called—"

"Bottle mats. We have them."

"Bottle mats. And a cash drawer. I'm tired of keeping all my money in a cigar box. And combs."

"Combs," said Keegan. "On an order this size, I'll be happy to throw in the combs and bottle mats gratis."

"Well, that's awful civil of you, friend."

"Glad to oblige," Keegan said, stifling the brief, bad thought that this was all an ugly joke; that in a second Craid and the boys would laugh in his face and run him out of town.

"Hey, Al," called the man in the chair, "I'm glad to hear you'll be fixing up this sty, but in the meantime I got soap drying on my face."

"Sure, Pete," said Craid. "Mr. Keegan, I don't want to drive off the custom here. Could I ask you to wait for a little—"

"Mr. Craid, I'd be happy to wait here till Thanksgiving. I'll just go through a catalog and mark things that I think will interest you."

"That's fine. I do thank you." Craid went back to the chair, slapped his razor against the strop, and started taking the lather off his customer's cheeks with sure, delicate strokes. Knows what he'd doing, Keegan thought; can jolly them and take good care of them too.

Dazed with heat and luck, Keegan sat down, opened a catalog, and leafed through it, marking the most expensive chairs, towel racks, and soap trays, but taking care to check off a good, middle-of-the-road oak mirror case.

He felt mellow about Craid, a nice man trying to build up his business. And, feeling mellow, he wanted to do well by the barber and was pleased at what he saw in the catalog. Kraut & Dohnal really did have a strong line. They weren't as gaudy as Koken, but Koken, trying to be so goddamned big, occasionally threw some trash in its catalog just for show. Kraut & Dohnal would never do that. If its best chair was quartersawn oak, and not enamel, it was still the best quartersawn oak money could buy, and made right there in the factory. Keegan knew for a fact that Koken got its precious enamel chairs from a jobber.

Keegan smiled into the catalog, while Charley and the others talked away, sometimes serious, sometimes merry. How they'd enjoy the model of the Congress Chair, when it came time to show it. Maybe on the strength of it, Craid would buy three. Keegan pulled a mechanical pencil from his vest, twisted the end to make the lead come out. It was clumsy and unpredictable, but people expected a drummer to have a snappy writing instrument. He scribbled some figures on the edge of the page next to the mirror case, checked them quickly, and saw that he stood to make a hundred dollars on this one sale. Then he licked his thumb and wiped his figuring to a blur; wouldn't do to have

Craid see it. The certainty of a hundred dollars softened the route still before him. Maybe they'd be as receptive down the line in St. Paul. Whatever happened, he'd be swinging back and forth through Hinckley now, helping Craid drive Turgeon out of business. Spend the night here now and again. Maybe see the dark-haired girl, Betty.

He thumbed through the catalog, drowsy with the busy click of Craid's scissors, and never noticed the sky going from gray to black outside the windows.

The other men in the shop did, though. One by one they left, going to see to their homes. Charley took a haircut, but waved away the shave and went out telling Keegan, "Go it, mister. Nick him the way he likes to nick us."

Keegan laughed, turned to Craid, and said, "Want to go over it now?"

Craid said he did, but he looked nervous. "Some wind."

"Man at the hotel told me it got this way every summer."

"Not like this." Craid wiped his hands on his jacket. "I've never seen it like this."

Keegan looked at the windows for the first time. "It's sure-to-God black out there."

Craid turned up the lights to their full 200 candlepower. "C'mon over here, why don't you, Mr. Keegan, and show me what you've got."

Keegan went through it, and Craid said he liked what he saw, but it was clear his heart wasn't in it. The wind thumped against the shop, and once Keegan thought he felt the floor shift underneath his feet.

"Can you write that up later, Mr. Keegan?" Craid asked. "I'd like to get on home myself. This is pretty bad."

"Why, certainly. But if—"

All the window glass flew in from the frames, and the ceiling caught fire. One of the Kraut & Dohnal lighting fixtures dropped to the floor. Spikes of flame stood outside the empty windows, then disappeared. In the darkness the wind blew the broken glass along the floor with a dry musical sound. Keegan took a step, slipped on the glass, and fell heavily on his back. He saw the oven glow of the ceiling, saw Craid's white jacket bob out the door.

"Wait!" he yelled, but the jacket was gone.

Keegan pressed his hands to the floor, felt the glass bite them, rolled with gingerly haste onto his stomach, and rose to his knees, then to his feet.

The ceiling gave off just enough light for him to make his way to the door. He stopped to pick up the model barber's chair; they'd charge him if he lost it. He stepped outside, and a wad of pitch slapped against his arm and clung burning to his sleeve. He scraped it off against the doorjamb. The shop ignited behind him, and he saw a rack lean down from the wall to spill its mugs. Clean white and gold, they sparkled as they fell.

This, a shrill, stupid little voice piped at him, is God's way of telling you to get out of the barber supply business.

He carried the model chair across the wooden sidewalk. The street was loud and black. He looked around and saw a lantern coming his way.

"Ha there!" he called.

The lantern went past, and wasn't a lantern at all, but a little girl, maybe nine or ten, with her dress on fire. Keegan dropped the chair and started after her. An explosion in the sky knocked him down. By the time he could get up, the street was dark again. He groped for the chair, couldn't find it, and then stood still, leaning into the scorching wind, wondering where to go.

A store across the way detonated and lit up the whole street. Keegan had thought he was the last person left in Hinckley, but dozens of men and women were running past, some of them burning. They all must have been screaming—their mouths were open—but he couldn't hear a thing except the wind and the loud chewing sound of the building consuming itself. Keegan stood and watched the hypnotic dumb show in the street with an absorption so vast he didn't even know it was terror.

A woman was pushing a baby along in a wildly jouncing wicker carriage, her arms stiff against the handle. A man holding what looked like a lunch pail overtook her, dashed past, and then just stopped and fell in the street. The carriage leaped over his legs and threw the baby out. The mother never broke step; she bounded along with the carriage, faster now that her cargo was gone.

The infant twitched and squirmed in a welter of blankets while men in heavy boots pounded past above it. The building was nearly gone, and in the last of its light Keegan, tugging himself along with the same reluctant muscles that had taken him into icy ponds when he was a boy, waded into the street and picked up the baby. Its face was cramped with rage, but when he got one hand under its bottom and another around its matchstick shoulders, it relaxed and opened wide eyes on him. The eyes shone red in the calm small face and Keegan, looking down at them, realized for the first time that he was almost certainly going to die.

He nearly threw the child away then, but it turned in his arms and he smelled its soapy hot smell. He hugged it to him, high up on his chest, and wasted time standing in the street while the last of the light died and the people ran past. They were just shadows now; it was too dark to see their open mouths.

A scrap of awning on the store went up and gave out a final flare that showed Keegan two things: an elegant sign, HARDWARE, with the long uprights of the letters erupting curlicues and edged in fresh gold leaf, and the dark-haired girl.

She was angling across the street toward him, her mouth closed but her eyes immense and her hair wild in the wind. Most of the people were running south, and she was working her way against them, shoulders hunched and arms loose at her sides, ready to check her fall if someone knocked her down.

The awning fell in a yellow gush, the street went black again, and Keegan, guessing, stuck out an arm, pulled in the person who struck it, and shouted, "Betty!"

She fell against him, put her mouth to his ear. He felt her lips say, "Father?"

"No. Keegan. The drummer."

Half a dozen explosions rattled nearby, sharp fast bangs like a string of firecrackers. The baby gave a single huge pulse and filled its hands with Keegan's hair. He held it, held Betty, and said, "Scott Keegan. Saw you while ago. Where you going?"

"Depot. Tommy."

Keegan heard only the word "Depot," guessed she knew something he didn't: "I'll go with you."

"But I can't see." Her mouth was still against his ear. "You have a baby."

Betty and the baby both moved aimlessly in his arms for a moment, then she cut loose and ran. He took hold of some part of her dress with his left hand and followed her. He lifted his feet high, always expecting to trip over something, but the street was flat and hard. The baby churned away under his chin, pulling his hair enough to hurt.

They ran in total darkness for what seemed to Keegan a long time. Then a delicate curtain of sparks came down, straight and leisurely despite the wind, and beyond the spark shower the ground lit up as the street ahead started to burn.

In the sudden light, Keegan saw the depot, long, low, and comforting with its peaked roof and telegraph bay, the building every drummer loved, the building you went through to leave town.

But the tracks in front of it were empty, save for a single freight car on a siding, blazing and shuddering.

"Betty, there's no train!"

She ran up the steps, and he followed her inside, where everything was bright because the whole southern wall was on fire, and part of the ceiling. Two small benches sat, stolid and pathetic, near the empty ticket office. A trick of the incoherent light made the ruby glass front of a gum-vending machine shine with almost holy splendor.

Beyond the shrine, a man was hammering away at the telegraph key. He didn't know Betty was there until she fell on his back, threw her arms around his chest, and shouted, "Tommy, Tommy, come away!" loud enough for Keegan to hear.

The telegrapher started and looked around—Keegan saw a bland young face with a self-conscious moustache—and Betty said, "Tommy, Tommy." He turned back to the key and she shook his shoulders.

"What in hell is all this?" Keegan asked the baby.

Tom Dunn had just nearly missed the last message he would ever receive. He was hot and weary, and still jangled from Betty's visit that morning, and when the chatterbox down at Pokegama started up again, he barely listened until the sounder gave out a particularly strange combination of letters. He scribbled then down, wondering whether he or Pokegama had gone wrong. Surely "doomed" couldn't be right; he'd never taken a word like "doomed."

Then Pokegama came back one more time: "Fire here. People dead. U next Hinckley."

Tom started asking questions, but Pokegama didn't answer. He threw the news out along the line; nobody answered.

He looked out through the bay window, saw the sole boxcar on the lay-by start to burn.

John Young, the depot agent, came into the bay, rubbing his hands on his vest the way he always did. He looked very worried just now, but he always looked very worried. He also served as the Adams Express Company agent, and Tom wondered if the double responsibility, which rewarded Young with an extra eleven dollars a month, was what made him seem so sad all the time.

"It's time we got out, Tom."

"We can't, John." Tom looked at the sounder, but it didn't say anything. "We got Jim Root coming in with the Number Four."

"Root'll be all right. Tom, we better get down to the Eastern depot. Best'll be there about now, and he'll be taking folks out. But he ain't going to wait forever. Tom, we're burning up here."

Young pointed to the southern wall. At first Tom didn't see anything wrong with it, but as he looked more closely he noticed the paint yellowing and crazing before his eyes.

Young rubbed his vest as though he were soaping himself. "Tom, it's about to go."

It went fast; the paint bulged into blisters and the fire was inside, running up to the ceiling. Chips of paint fell, each carrying a little barb of flame.

"You come now, Tom!"

Tom waved him away, swung back to the key. "You go, John, I'll come in a minute."

Young stamped out the small fires the paint chips had scattered across the floor. "Tom, you don't even know if that line's still live."

Dunn didn't look up from the key. "And you don't know it's not."

"Tom, you got to come now. It's got to the ceiling and once the—"

But Tom wasn't listening to Young; he was thinking of the night Sy Hornby got drunk and put the freight on the line with the limited. It had been just this dark outside the bay, with lightning flaring almost the way the fire was now. Before Sy had walked out to do whatever he was going to do for the rest of his life he had told Tom it was no ribbon clerk's job, telegraphy.

Tom had wanted to drive locomotives, but somehow he'd never gotten there; maybe being a railroad man wouldn't mean so much to him if he had. Come to that, he wasn't even a very good lightning slinger. Sy had told him he'd never be fast, just competent.

Old Schwertfeger had been competent, had stayed at the key while the consumption made him cough his lungs out, little by little, into the back of his hand. Sy Hornby had been twice as fast as Schwertfeger, but Schwertfeger had never killed anybody. Tom would probably go out like Schwertfeger, not Hornby; one day he'd be old Dunn, getting a little slow, but always punctual, a reliable home guard on the St. Paul & Duluth.

Outside the bay, the boxcar was just about gone. Ties were afire before and behind it, but everything else was blackness. The car seemed to be dying on a miraculous bridge.

Behind the car, somewhere up the main line, Root was coming with the Number Four Limited. Tom had no love for Root—the bleak old fart would sooner part with a double-eagle gold piece than a common pleasantry—but Root would certain sure be bringing in his train, and somebody had to be on hand to clear it.

Young was working his vest so vigorously that Tom was surprised he hadn't rubbed the buttons off. "John, you go now. I'm sticking here until Root gets in."

"Tom, goddamnit, *look* out there. Root ain't coming!"

"Well, if he doesn't get here, it won't be my fault."

The whole building groaned. Young gave his vest a final, convulsive rub, opened his mouth, shut it, and ran for the door.

Tom worked the key, trying to pretend it was like any other trick, until he could feel the fire at his back.

When Betty fell on him, it scared him half to death. She yelled his name and, flustered, he turned back to the key. She clung to him, pulling at his shoulders, telling him he had to come save himself. And there was somebody else in the room, a man with a baby, looking like any father about to go off on a trip, except he was dressed much too sharp, and the baby's mother wasn't with him, and he was staring stupidly at the new gum machine.

Betty kept tugging at him. He could feel the strength in her sturdy, frightened body. She was big and lovely and she'd come to save his life. "Tom, people are burning up!"

He looked into her face, thought of the taffy pull where he'd first gotten up the courage to talk to her, thought of the morning in her yard after the wreck. And he thought of the man who'd caused the wreck.

"It's no ribbon clerk's job, Betty. I can't leave. You get down to the Eastern depot and get on that train."

She shook her head. "I'm not leaving until you do."

Tom turned to the man with the baby. "Mister, will you get her out of here? Get over to the other depot. They'll take you out."

The man wanted to know where the other depot was. Tom told him it was just down the street, and to hurry up. Betty said she wouldn't stir.

Flakes of fire started to fall from the ceiling.

"Mister, take her away!"

The man ran out the door.

"Hell! Betty, please follow him."

"Only if you come too."

They looked at each other across a wind that took all the orders off the desk; the south wall had fallen.

"Betty, go to the Eastern. Go to the depot. You'll die for sure if you stay here."

"No."

"Betty, it'd never be different, even if I came. It'd always be just the way it's been with us. Anyway, I can't leave."

The man came back in. He no longer had the baby.

"Hello," Tom called giddily, "good to see you again."

He came over, moving his mouth slackly above his awful suit, took

Betty under the arms, lifted her up, and slapped her hard. "Come along," he said.

She never looked back at Tom; the man helped her out through the door with the tough delicacy of someone guiding a senile maiden aunt through a family funeral.

"Thank you," Tom shouted, but they were gone. He'd been away from the key too long. He worked it fast, then, worked it as well as Sy Hornby ever had. He slapped messages out over the dead wire until the fire got to the big crossbeams that held up the roof.

Billy Toback disappeared, and that was the last Jemmy ever saw of him. They'd been running along together, heads down against the falling sparks, until a tree flashed like a photographer's magnesium tray right in front of them. Jemmy turned, gasping, and Billy was gone.

Jemmy thought of going back, but the tree burned itself out, darkness came down again, and he cut for home. He couldn't see anything, but he knew the backyard topography of his town as only a small boy can. He could run blind from anywhere to anywhere in Hinckley.

He angled across the Lubbocks' yard, jumped the small gully that ran along the eastern boundary of his mother's garden, figured he was only a few yards away from the privy now. "Mommy! Daddy!" he called, which he knew was silly because the wind was so loud, but he kept shouting as he made for the back door of his house.

Fire bloomed in the sky for a moment and the smoke thinned and Jemmy saw there was no house there. The cellar was a bin of bright rubble that seemed to reflect the flame overhead. A black oval shifted and sank into the embers as Jemmy watched: the dining room table.

"Mommy," he said. "Daddy."

He ran back across the Lubbocks' yard to the road. It was dark again now, and once something hot and heavy hit his back and knocked him down. When he got up, there was the St. Paul & Duluth depot in front of him, looking just like it always did except the roof was on fire. A man came out the door carrying a baby and shouted at him. Generally a grown-up shouting meant trouble, but Jemmy was awful glad to see this one. He went over to him. "Good afternoon," he said. He knew it sounded funny under the circumstances, but that's how his mother had taught him to address strangers.

"Hello, son." The man crouched down and looked in his face. "Where you going?"

"I'm looking for Mommy—for my mother and father."

"They're not at home?"

"My home's gone. I went there and it's all burned up. So I don't know where they are."

"Oh." A burning book blew up the street, throwing out puffs of sparks every time it hit the ground.

The man looked sad and scared. Jemmy said, "I'm Jemmy Stockholm."

"Scott Keegan." He started to stick out his hand, but fumbled the baby and grabbed it. "You look to be a likely boy, Jemmy, and I think I know where your parents are. I think they're down at the other depot. Do you know where that is?"

"Of course. Everybody does."

"Good. There's a train down there, going to take everybody away. Now you just go down and get on that train and you'll find them sooner or later. Understand?"

Jemmy nodded.

"Good. Now, I want you to do me a favor. I want you to take this baby along with you. I can't keep it. Here, take hold of it. Doesn't weigh much at all."

Jemmy didn't remember ever having held a baby, but it didn't seem too hard when the man passed it to him. "Just keep an arm under its behind and don't worry if it makes a fuss. Babies are always making a fuss about something."

The baby was at once lighter and solider than Jemmy would have guessed. It didn't have any teeth at all.

"Where's the train going?"

"What's the difference? It's going out of here."

"I don't have any money for the fare."

"I don't think they'll be worrying about that today." But the man fished in his pocket, pulled out a bill, and handed it to him.

The baby jabbed its fist at Jemmy's eye with brutal determination. The man rose to his feet.

"Good luck, boy."

"Mister! Mister! This here's ten dollars!"

"That's fine. You can take the baby for a holiday in New York City after you get him out of here." The man waved and ran back into the depot. That didn't make any sense to Jemmy. The baby started making a creaking noise.

"Quiet," said Jemmy. He wrapped his arms around the infant and ran down the street, past the milliner's store where the single mannequin stood scowling in the window with her dress and hair burning.

When the people finally came, they came all at once, screaming and crowding.

"Why'n hell weren't they here earlier?" Barry asked Thistle, who didn't know. Barry was sick of waiting. First he'd had to wait for Best to get in, then he'd had to wait while Best took on water—you'd think the man had had to build the tank first, the time it took him—and then, by God, he'd had to wait while Best niggled around the freight yard picking up three boxcars and a caboose, and coupled them onto Barry's train. Was Best ready to leave then? Nosir. Best's horrible Yankee conductor, Hiram Powers, had to come dawdling back and say in his horrible Yankee voice through his horrible Yankee nose, "We'll be waiting, Mr. Barry, for folks to be along." There were no folks, just buildings catching fire, closer and closer.

Barry didn't want to skedaddle while a veteran like Best was waiting, but he was just about to when Powers came back and said they were hooking up the air and Best would be in charge of the brakes. "What do I do?" Barry wanted to know, and Powers said, in his whickering way, that Barry was to wait on Best's word, and move like lightning when it came.

"Why's that? Why do I have to wait for Best?"

"Because"—Powers made three syllables out of it, "becaw-was"—"Best is senior to you, and I'm senior to ever'body."

So Barry waited, watching Thistle pick nervously at his teeth under the close, dismal light of the cab lamps, and now and again glancing out the window to see the fire coming nearer.

The engines stood nose to tail with the cars between them: Barry's locomotive at the rear facing the five coaches, then the three boxcars Best had picked up, and the caboose, and finally Best's tender and engine.

"You know," Barry said suddenly to his fireman, "you know, we'll be backing out when the time comes. Best can't make me do a goddamn thing. We'll be at the head of this train. We can just cut loose and back away when we please, Alex."

Thistle scooped coal into the firebox. "You'd've backed out an hour ago if that was true."

"If I got to, I got to," said Barry. "I'm not going to sit here while Best gets me killed."

"I wish we were canal men," said Thistle.

Then all the people came. Barry never saw them coming, just saw them there, flailing against the sides of the cars. The first man aboard sat in a wheelchair. Two draymen lifted him into a boxcar and climbed in after him. After that, Gilham and McLaughlin, Barry's brakemen, helped the refugees into the train.

At first it went well. The brakemen handed the women up, then lifted their children to them. But soon the sky came down, a thick tensile bulging like sheet iron being bent, and fire dripping down through joints in it. The fire touched people in the crowd, and instantly they were consumed. They grabbed at their neighbors as they fell. A man pulled off his jacket and tried to beat out the dress of a woman who was thrashing at his feet; but the fire ran up his coat and in seconds he was dying on the ground beside her. After that, the crowd drew away from the burning people, gave them a seven-foot circle to kick out their lives in.

"That's enough!" screamed Barry. "We're full up! We got to leave!"

He whistled to Best, opened the throttle, and felt the slack being taken up in the cars behind him as the train got under way. "Here we go, Alex!" he sang out, and then the slack ran out and he was pitched up against a hot pipe and burned hell out of his hand.

"We stopped," said Thistle. "What happened?"

"I burned my hand," said Barry, and started to cry.

Best was out talking with Powers about how long they could stick around when he saw his engine being pulled back past him. He leaped for the gangway, swung himself in by the cab post, and yanked the brake handle.

Ford, who was peering into the firebox making sure the flues weren't tearing holes in the fire, stuck out a gloved hand and braced himself as the brakes took hold and the train bumped to a halt.

"That son of a bitch Barry," said Best, still hanging on the brake, "tried to run us out of here."

Campbell climbed to the cab. "Barry says to tell you he's going to pull the coupling pin and go."

"I guess not." Best didn't think he'd shouted, but Campbell backed right off.

"I'll go tell him he has to stick—wasn't my idea to pull out, Mr. Best." Campbell jumped out of the cab.

The engine tilted to the left.

"The bastard trying it again?" Best held fast to the brake handle. "He didn't even whistle!"

"Nope," said Ford. "That's the ties going. Rails're starting to spread."

Best looked out his cab, saw the people piling in and behind them a team coming down the street, both horses and burning like horses in a fairy tale. The driver vaulted from his rig, ran a dozen paces, and dropped. It was so dark that if the horses hadn't been burning, Best wouldn't have seen him at all.

He turned to his fireman. "Barry's damn well right."

Ford, judiciously sprinkling coal into his firebox, didn't look up. "If you say so."

Best hit him on the shoulder. "Stop it, George! What do you say?"

Ford propped his scoop against the back head. "I say it's up to Powers."

"That's right." Best felt a panicky sort of relief. They might all die; he might die; but it wouldn't be his fault. Powers was in charge. Best sat back. He didn't have a thing to do. But after a while he reached forward and rested his hand on the throttle. No point wasting time when the word came.

Best was working hard at doing nothing when some citizen stuck his head into the cab. The man was screaming so vigorously that all Best saw was white eyes and a straw hat. "Get out!" the man screamed. "Get out, everybody's on!" Before Best could say anything, the man's hat lifted in the air; the crown went in a sprinkle of hot red grains, and the brim spun forward along the boiler. Best watched it go, saw that the press of people had thinned.

Here and there men and women were coming around the depot, heading for the train, but few of them made it; they dropped and burned. Best couldn't see any fire on them as they fell, but they went up fast once they were on the ground.

The citizen had disappeared with his hat. The street was empty. Up ahead, Barry kept whistling—two long blasts, a second's pause, two more blasts: move out, move out. The whistle came back to Best thin and whimsical through the wind.

No sign of Powers. A pile of shingles that some farmer hadn't bothered to pick up when they came in a week ago clattered into flame, and Best saw a boy running past them. The boy held a bundle—a baby. He fell, and the baby bounced along the ground ahead of him. Best looked away.

Someone shook his shoulder: Powers, his conductor's cap still prim on his head. "Better go, Bill. The ties're on fire."

Best whistled twice, and barely got the throttle open before Barry had taken up the slack again, and they were moving.

Jemmy Stockholm lay on his stomach and was cool where he lay. He'd been blown over by a hot buffeting wind, but down on the street it wasn't so bad.

There were women on fire in the street near him, and one of them was his mother's friend Mrs. Gresham, who had come by the night before for some berries. She opened her mouth so wide he could see the pink ribs in her throat. Even her purse was burning.

A smooth thing turned inside Jemmy's head, turned upward from the back of his neck and down over his eyes glib as a silver ice cream scoop, so that he could see Mrs. Gresham, see the other ladies, but his head was cool and he was cool, down in the dust.

Mrs. Gresham's face pulled away from her teeth until she was all smile and no eyes.

He'd dropped the baby.

It was there in front of him, in front of the burning women, on its back with its arms in the air. He went for it, hooking himself forward on his elbows because he was scared to stand up in that wind.

When he got to the baby he saw its mouth was open, but he couldn't hear its squalling because the wind was making a noise like wagons being driven fast over a bad road.

Jemmy put a hand on the baby and lay beside it wondering if he had the pluck to get to his feet and make a run. The train wasn't far; when the dirty, guttering light flared, he could see it right ahead of him, its red boxcars homey and solid. People were getting on, and steam was rising, thick and luminous, from two locomotives. Soon the train would take the people away from the fire, and take Jemmy to his parents if he could get on. But the sky was so loud, and Mrs. Gresham was dead right next to him.

The train started moving, backing slowly away. Jemmy knew trains always started slow, but then were suddenly going fast. He got to his feet and the sky let him stay there. He snatched up the baby and ran for the train. It was already picking up speed.

Jemmy squeezed the baby to his chest, closed his eyes, and pounded toward the cars. When he opened his eyes he was no closer. He closed them again and kept running, and the next time he looked the last boxcar was moving past right in front of him and a man was leaning way out through the door, reaching for him.

Gilham, the brakeman, had been trying to get people to stay still when they finally pulled out. He was the only trainman in the car and he'd never handled passengers before. He wasn't doing well. "Keep still or you'll all die," he kept yelling, which he thought should quiet anybody down, but every time he yelled it they all rucked around, and there must have been two hundred of them. "*Please* keep still or you'll all die," he shouted, but even that didn't help.

They fell down when the train started up. That kept them busy for a couple of seconds, but then a flaming branch blew in the door and they started shoving and kicking again. He heard somebody scream, "Get the goddamn women out!"

Gilham went to slide the door shut, and there was a kid running for the train, holding a bundle. The grab iron was gone—the pissing maintenance bums earned as much as brakemen, never did squat—so he took hold of the doorpost and stretched out his arm until he was nearly touching the boy. The sleepy little bastard had his eyes closed.

"Hey! Hey, kid!"

The kid couldn't hear him.

"Hey!"

The kid opened his eyes.

"Run," screamed Gilham, but the engineers were hightailing now and the boy couldn't keep up.

Gilham hooked a heel into the door track, swung out wide, and grabbed. He got the kid's wrist, lost it, and took hold of a coverall strap. The moment he got it the kid sagged and Gilham had to drag him in ass first. He dropped the boy on the floor and slammed the door closed. If there was another kid out there, it could look after itself. Then, even though the passengers were wailing again, Gilham just lay down and breathed for a while.

"Mister, mister, is he alive?"

The kid was shoving a baby in Gilham's face. It looked like any other baby: ugly, inconsequential, and full of life.

"Baby's fine, Jack. He's in better shape than I am."

"Mister, sir, I have the fare." Holding the baby in one arm, the kid fished in a pocket and produced a ten-dollar bill.

The brakeman looked at the boy and the baby, then took the money.

"Is that enough?" the boy asked anxiously.

"That'll just exactly cover the cost of the ride for you and your friend."

Somebody in the black, teeming car called, "Trainman, there's a sick woman here!"

"That's terrible," said Gilham. He stuck the ten in his pocket and lay back down by the door.

As he backed out of Hinckley, Best leaned from his cab for a last look. A house was burning so rapidly that the walls seemed to melt away, and he could see into someone's bedroom. There was a sturdy oak dresser with a coffee cup on it, a shirt hanging over a half-open closest door, a pitcher in a bowl, a night table with a molten square of mirror above it. Later, he'd remember the hellish intimacy of that bedroom more clearly than the men and women dying yards away from his train. But just then it only reminded him that his wife had left four thimbles out on her work table the night before, and what did she need with all those thimbles?

Then he thought of the nineteen bridges he had to cross. Every one of them was made of wood.

After Keegan had slapped Betty and pulled her from the depot, she followed him readily enough through the howling darkness. The street was empty now, and the fire had come by because Keegan could feel the hot ground through his shoe leather. A burning stretch of wooden sidewalk showed him two corpses in the street, both so charred he couldn't tell their sex as he glanced at them. One had been carrying silverware; it lay like jackstraws around the body.

Betty dropped back. He turned and saw her standing over the bodies, covering her mouth with her hands. "Come on!" He took her arm. She ran beside him past the glowing skeletons of buildings to where the blazing Eastern Minnesota depot lit up the empty tracks in front of it.

Keegan pulled her to a halt. She put an arm around his shoulder and leaned against him sobbing. He shook her. "Where's the train? Betty, where's the train?"

She pointed up the tracks to some burning debris—a stump, a pump house? Keegan squinted through the smoke. It was the stack of a locomotive. It disappeared around a bend and the north was dark again.

"Now what?"

Betty shook her head.

"Come on, you *live* here!"

"There's nowhere to go. We're going to die."

"Hell with that kind of talk!" He looked around. Fire rose like a sudden dawn, streaked and red, where the train had gone. Fire was all around them.

"It looks lowest over there." He took her hand and pulled her back the way they'd come, past the gutted shops and the corpse with its knives and forks and teaspoons.

It was Gettysburg all right: the smoke, the noisy sky, too much to do too quickly, febrile death at your elbow in a thousand small poppings and hurryings. Chief Craig bellowed through the smoke, and Alex Rosedahl and Horace Gorton joined Peterson and Barrett at the nozzle. Men from the Brennan mill lurched back and forth with barrels of water. The air was full of fire, fierce gossamer sheets of it that kited around head-high before being sucked back up into the low clouds. One jiggled down toward the nozzlemen, and they bent up the hose to smash it in the air.

"Stop that!" Craig shouted. "Keep that water on the ground. You two men, bring your barrels near the crew and stand by to douse them if they get hit."

Hit. That made no sense in firefighting. But the barrelmen understood and trundled their kegs over to the boys at the nozzle. Craig satisfied himself that they were close enough to do the job, then looked around, opened his vision to the broader scene just as he had on Culp's Hill half a lifetime ago. First the particular terror, then the general terror.

All around, fire was spouting out of the ground, great gobs of it rising from the earth, one after the other, like the white-hot spewing of Roman candles. Some of the fireballs burst as they rose, others bounced along the ground. One glided placidly through the sky to brush across a barrelman's head. Instantly the man was sheathed in fire. He jumped and spun, and the nozzlemen knocked him over with their stream, but it was too late.

"Forget him!" The men were watching the smoking corpse while the hose drilled uselessly into the ground at their feet. "Forget him. Hit that!" Craig pointed to a new fire fifty feet away. Barrett leveled the nozzle around, walked the water over the fire, and as the steam geysered up it turned green. The whole sky turned green for a moment; the feathered joinings of the low clouds radiated a calm underwater light. The light made it all seem like a storm at sea, despite the dry furnace blast of the wind. Then the clouds closed in on each other and everything was black and red again.

A line of fire zipped up from the west to stand straight and solid as a board fence. Craig saw a man come crawling through it on his hands and knees, his feet trailing garters. The nozzlemen started in on the near end of the fire as the man worked his way toward Craig. He slumped forward and lay still, head in his arms, buttocks in the air. The garters were long calf tendons, burned away from the bone as he came through the fire.

Father Lawler ran to the man and knelt beside him. Craig saw the priest saying some of his heathen mumbo jumbo, but obviously the man was gone. Lawler crossed himself, then straightened the man out and turned him over. He got up and came over to Craig.

"Doesn't look good."

Craig glanced over his shoulder to where a dull yellow patch in the smoke signaled the end of Hinckley.

Craig shook his head. They weren't fighting to save the town anymore; they were fighting to save their lives. He looked toward the nozzlemen and saw a horrible thing: Barrett had his hand half over the nozzle to make the water go farther. If the engine were working properly, passing your hand through that stream would be no easier than passing it through a connecting rod. Craig ran to the engine. It was working fine, ticking away like a dollar watch. So what was the—he looked up the length of hose that lay between the engine and the nozzlemen and saw half a dozen tiny white parasols rising from it. Sparks had burned through the canvas, letting out little jets of water.

He could have patched one, could have patched two, but this was too many. And even as he watched, another sprouted. He ran to the boys working the nozzle. Barrett still had his hand over it, but now the wind was blowing the water right back in the firemen's faces.

Craig swatted Barrett on the shoulder and the druggist turned an empty, terrified face to him.

"It's over, Noble. We got to try and save ourselves."

"Do we pull off the engine, Chief?"

Craig shut his eyes. "No," he said, "there's no time. We got to go."

"Go where?" Peterson asked, and Craig had no answer. He thought. Grindstone Creek would be too low, the millpond was too far, the swamp would be too dry. He remembered the Eastern Minnesota's controversial eyesore.

"The gravel pit! Go to the gravel pit. Run!"

They dropped the hose and started off. Craig went to tell the barrelmen and the boys who were stoking the engine. Fire was streaming from the sky now; you couldn't tell if the ground was throwing flame up or the sky was throwing it down. Craig tapped the last man, a skinny little mill hand who was crouching behind his barrel as though someone were shooting at him. The man took to his heels and Craig ran to where his horse was rearing and frothing and bucking at the rope that tethered it to a stump. At first he thought he wouldn't be able to mount, but after some frantic soothing the beast calmed enough to let him on its back. He sawed at the reins, turned toward the gravel pit, and then squandered enough time for a final look at his beautiful new engine.

All four wheels were burning. Craig could see the new varnish blister; and as he watched, the spokes gave way and the engine fell on its side, the pierced hose still weakly pumping water.

LeMoyne had no idea where he was, how he'd gotten there, or where he should go. He's been in his hotel room writing up his orders for the fire engine watches while the wind shook the window. Then people suddenly were running in the hallways screaming fire, and he was going downstairs. Somehow the banister had caught fire, though the lobby was undamaged. He supposed that was what was causing all the stir until he got out the door onto the monstrous street. He'd barely time to take in the fact that the whole town was going up when a shop sign came sailing through the air, caught him in the neck, and knocked him cold.

His wife was talking to him, right next to his ear; talking in a quiet voice but telling him to get up fast, get up and get out before your back hurts more. His face was in the dirt and there was something heavy on his back. He opened his eyes and saw his head in elongated silhouette; someone was sitting on his back and shining a lantern to make it cast a shadow. The pressure turned to pain. He was on fire. He rolled over on his back, but that didn't help enough. A boot appeared in front of his face, vanished. People were running by. Hooves. He was in a thicket of horse legs, saw with wonderful acuity a worn horseshoe with one nail gone and another all but gone. Then something final and terrible hit him, squeezed the air out of him. He saw the wagon going away; it seemed so tall it might have been flying through the air with the driven cinders. He knew he had to get out of the road, but his legs were out of whack. His arms worked but there was nothing he could grab to pull himself along. He was too heavy to make much headway with his elbows, but he got a few yards before he had to rest and close his eyes.

His wife had fixed a roast of beef, and fried potatoes, with a big tureen of apple butter, which didn't exactly go with the meal, but he loved it. She stood at the head of the table looking sad. She was very far away and it was pathetic that she'd spent so much time on the meal.

His grandfather poked him in the stomach. "Oh, you're a fat little boy. I have a present for you, do you know where it is?" He picked at a big brown hairy wen on the back of his grandfather's hand. "Is it in there?" It wasn't, and everybody got embarrassed.

It was dark now. There was a man in the street near him with his hair all gone, his eyes half open.

"Afternoon," said LeMoyne.

The man stared and stared.

"Two drunks," said LeMoyne, "sitting on the curb, looking at a mangy old dog. Fleas, sore. Dog's curled up, licking his balls.

"One drunk says, 'Sure wish I could do that.' "

He wasn't telling the story very well, wasn't giving it enough of a buildup, which was bad because then they thought all you wanted was to hurry through the joke and sell them something.

"And his friend says, 'You better pet him a little first.' "

The man didn't get it, or didn't like it. Well, he hadn't made much of a job telling it. But you can't expect a man to be funny all the time.

Bull Henly, the St. Paul & Duluth section boss at Hinckley, had never been too frightened in his life, and he wasn't frightened now. He was mad, though.

The waste was what made him mad. He spent his life keeping the St. P. & D. tracks around Hinckley in good shape, and now a shapeless, formless noisy catastrophe had wrecked it all. Killed his best man, too, Warren. Henly had seen him burn up. The rest of the boys had run off.

Henley had dawdled around the line for a while with the woods hooing and banging around him, but there wasn't a damn thing to do. Root was due through and he could have flagged Root down, but now the tracks were gone clear to the depot and it was gone too, and Root would find that out by himself.

So Henly started down toward the Eastern Minnesota depot to see if anything needed doing there. It was a bad walk and it made him madder. There were little girls all burned up in the street, men and women, and the fat drummer who'd sold the firemen their watches yesterday.

Henly had sat on his temper for years. He was very big, and it was too easy to kill people when you got mad, and then they put your ass in jail forever, and that was the end of fixing the track and ragging the boys, of pie-eating contests and beer. But now his town was gone and his track was wrecked and the people who said "Morning, Bull" were dead in the street with their families, and it all made him so mad he wasn't scared.

There was nothing to do at the Eastern, either, by the time he got there. The depot was just finishing burning down and the tracks had curled right up in the air.

The depot burned itself out. It got dark, and Henly stood there. He didn't have a thing to do.

Because of the wind, he saw the horse before he heard it. He yelled, and the man on the horse reined in as best he could; the horse kept dancing around and trying to step sideways.

"Who's that?"

"Bull. It's me, Bull. That you, Craig?"

"Bull, get to the gravel pit!"

"Why?"

"Get in the water. It's your only chance."

Craig rode off. Henly felt better because now he had something to do. He trotted over to the pit and posted himself in the road right near a gully that ran down to the water. A man pounded by with his trouser legs burning, and Henly grabbed him.

"Let go!" The man looked crazy.

"Gravel pit!" Henly shouted in his face, and pushed him down the gully.

A woman came next, came up to him cautiously, as though she didn't want to bother him. "Could you help me?" she asked politely.

"Yes ma'am," said Henly, "just go down there and get in the water."

"Thank you," she said.

Then people came in a bunch, and Henly didn't have time to talk with them, he just stuck out his arms and shouted, "There! There!" until they were all in the pit.

He liked shouting at a lot of people better than just helping individuals, because he was so mad.

After the bunch of people had got into the water, a man came up to Henly and asked what he was doing.

"Get in there," said Henly, and pointed down the gully.

The man wouldn't go. "You helping people into the pit?" he asked. Henly recognized him.

"You the fish-eater minister?"

"That's right," said Father Lawler.

"Well, you better get in, too."

"Maybe," said the priest, "I'll go over there and help you out."

"Suit yourself," said Henly. The man went off, cool as a cucumber. Henly's father had told him a lot of awful bad things about the fish eaters, but this one didn't seem so bad.

Lawler went a hundred yards south to another street and got there in time to intercept a Swedish family—father, mother, three squalling children—who were running back into the town.

"Stop!"

They did, but they couldn't speak English and he couldn't speak

Swedish, so he had to lead them over to Henly, who shoved them into the water.

When he got back to his post, Lawler found a mob milling around. "Go to the gravel pit," he shouted, and someone shouted back, "To hell with that!"

It was Peter Grimes, a member of his small congregation.

"Stop it, Peter. Go to the gravel pit. Chief Craig says it's our best chance."

"The swamp!" shouted Grimes, and they all ran past Lawler, even though he yelled and yelled. He stopped when he heard himself yelling, ". . . defying the will of God!" That was very wrong, trying to get people to do something he wanted them to do by invoking God, and worse still that he'd done it without even thinking. He knew he wasn't a proud man, but there was a difference between lack of pride and humility. A truly humble man wouldn't start quacking about God's will just because he was in a tight spot. If God wanted the crowd of people with Grimes to survive the fire in the swamp, then they would.

Grimes and the others ran north through the town up the old wagon road toward the swamp. They remembered the swamp from autumn duck hunting when it was a place of bogs and moss and black water coming up around your feet. They got safely past the feeble trickle of Grindstone Creek, got in along the swamp's tall trees, but found the ground dry and springy underfoot. They were still seeking wet autumn hollows when fire spread flat and low over the sky and pulled the breath from their lungs, sucked a huge, fluting wail from one hundred and twenty-six people and left them dead even before the heat burned away all their clothing but the soles of their shoes and shrank them to four-foot-tall-mummies.

Keegan thought he and Betty were the last people left alive in Hinckley until he came to the St. Paul & Duluth tracks and saw scores of men, women, and children running north. North seemed no worse than any other choice; the flames were all around the horizon now.

He pulled at Betty's arm. She gave him a vacant look, but stuck close by as he plunged into the mob. At first they ran along the ties, but the going was too rough and twice Keegan tripped. After a couple of hundred yards the roadbed widened a little and he and Betty could run beside the tracks.

For a while it was dark and Keegan knew he was in a crowd only by the dry grunting and the slap of feet against the cinder bed. Then, suddenly, a clearing to the left of the tracks lit up like a music hall stage, and Keegan saw the last seconds of the Brennan mill.

A thunderclap of hot wind lifted the roof off a long, low building, and the boards came apart—opened like slats in a blind—to show a white-hot interior and the orderly black silhouettes of heavy machinery. An immense band saw came unsprung, fell in flashing coils, and then the roof dropped, knocked the sides flat, and sent sparks gusting toward the tracks.

Betty started screaming and Keegan saw her dress was afire. She tried to run from it, but Keegan seized her by the waist and threw her to the ground. She fought him, eyes closed. She was very strong. He sat on her stomach, took hold of her skirt in both hands, tore it off at the waist, and was absurdly shocked to see her fine long legs, pink in the light from the dying sawmill.

What'd you expect? he said to himself as he helped her to her feet. She opened her eyes, looked down at her bare legs, and for the first time since they'd left the depot he saw some kind of comprehension come over her face. "Thank you," she said. She glanced at the mill and at the people running past them along the tracks. "I don't want to die," she said in a firm, slightly wondering way, as if she'd surprised herself by coming to a brave and difficult decision.

"Me neither," said Keegan. "Come on."

They ran together into an endless gauntlet. Beyond the mill clearing the trees closed in around the right-of-way, forcing them back onto the tracks. Keegan found he could fit his stride to the ties for two or three hundred feet at a time, but then the heat and the wind would sap his concentration and he'd falter. Betty did better than he did. For a while she ran along beside him, and then she pulled ahead a bit, so that her legs with their silly black shoes rose and fell, rose and fell, white in the darkness.

Every so often there would be an explosion off in the woods, sharp and sudden as a shell burst, and the flare would lay black bands across the tracks and cast a red glow on the people struggling along. The wind was at Keegan's back; otherwise, he couldn't have kept his eyes open.

Keegan had gone about a mile, he guessed, when a thick rope of flame lashed out of the woods and took down a woman fifty feet ahead. She dropped as soon as it hit her and rolled flaming off the tracks. By the time Keegan ran past her she was completely incinerated. A few seconds later another gout of flame took the man directly behind him. People were dying all up and down the track; sometimes Keegan had to jump over their bodies.

His lungs had hot little holes in them and he couldn't take a breath. If he'd ever had a second wind, he's burned it out way back down the line. His legs were light, but moved slowly as though he were bouncing along through water. He felt his mind begin to slip. After a while he started to worry about the expensive model barber chair. They'd dock him plenty for that. He'd had such a stinking season it might even cost him his job. Then where would he be?

Maybe he had a second wind after all. It wasn't so hard to run. In fact, it wasn't anything to run. Burning corpses jerked back past him as if they were moving by on a long, gritty belt and he were standing watching them. It was nice not to work so hard, but the chair nagged him. How could he have let it get away from him? After carrying it ten thousand miles, he'd thrown it away like so much rubbish.

He almost wept with relief when he saw the chair lying by the tracks, its polished nickel fittings glittering red in the mordant light.

He stepped off the tracks, stopped running, vomited up a thin, sour liquid. When he was through retching, he couldn't find the chair. It must be farther from the tracks than he'd thought. He wasn't going to let it get away from him a second time.

He was heading into the woods when someone took his arm and pulled him back. It was Betty, with her bare legs and dark hair. "What are you doing?" she screamed at him.

Well, he was only looking for the chair, he told her, but words wouldn't come. He made the words with his mouth, but all he could get was a sandy, scraping sound.

"Hurry!"

He shook his head. Not till he found the chair. He turned from her and she spun him back around and hit him in the eye with her closed fist.

"Ow!" There was his voice.

"You're crazy. We have to get back to the tracks."

He rubbed his eye and his ears shrilled a piping note that ascended into silence. He heard the deep, steady crashing noise of the burning forest. Christ's sake, he'd left the goddamned chair back in town. He'd just about gone and . . .

Betty was tugging him back toward the tracks. "Hurry, I don't want to lose you, too."

"Jesus, thanks for stopping." He took her hand and they rejoined the mob on the tracks.

They ran forever, Betty out ahead again, and he puked a second time without breaking step. Fire kept coming out of the trees, people kept dying. He ran for a long time over burning ties, and didn't know why he was still alive. He began to feel a thin, petulant anger at Betty for keeping him from going into the woods. He was a dead man anyway; why hadn't she let him get it over with?

The white legs moved like machinery. How the hell did she keep it up? He marked a tall tree wearing a plume of flame some three hundred feet ahead. He'd go that far and no more. Blue-green specks turned slowly in front of his eyes. He could see the tree beyond them, getting closer, its branches lashed by the wind but only the crest burning. He should tell Betty he was going to call it quits, but he couldn't get abreast of her and he probably wouldn't have had the breath to speak if he did.

There. He passed the tree, gave it an extra thirty feet, and sat down. He watched Betty running along. He hoped she wouldn't notice he'd dropped out; she might come back for him again. Damn, but she had sand, that one.

He'd never see her again. The thought made him try to stand, but his legs just wouldn't hold him. He waved to her dwindling back.

The pale, fixed beam of a locomotive headlight swept around the bend. Christ, I'm seeing things again, he thought; now I think there's a special train bringing back my chair. But the crowd had stopped running, and Betty had stopped, too.

The St. Paul & Duluth was a good road to work for; a man could do just about as he pleased so long as he pulled the trains. For Jack McGowan this meant that firemen didn't have to do too much cleaning. In fact, Jack had never once polished any cab brasses—until he started firing for Root.

Root was the real item. He'd been driving locomotives almost since they'd been invented, and Jack had never met a man who knew more about the business. But he was a terrible stickler for tidiness. Where other firemen wiped the jackets about once a week, Jack had to wipe off Number Sixty-nine every day, as well as blackening the front and the stack, a chore he loathed. To add to his irritation, the other firemen guyed him: called him and ass-kisser and accused him of trying to get them to work harder.

Jack had felt badly used for some time, but it wasn't quite clear to him why he'd chosen this particular day for his mutiny. Maybe it was the smear of low gray cloud that had sealed the heat in over Duluth for weeks; maybe it was only that he'd slept badly the night before. But when Jack got to the yard Saturday morning he built his fire and then just sat in the cab. The locomotive looked fine to him—he'd wiped it yesterday—but he knew Root would find it pretty scabby. And Root had been in a particularly grim mood the day before. He'd been favoring his right arm, too. Jack guessed there was something wrong with it. After a nervous, idle hour, Jack decided the hell with it, he'd black the old bastard's stack after all. Just then, though, Root appeared, got into his overclothes, and started around with the long can, oiling. So Jack stayed in the cab, the way he'd planned, full of misgivings.

Root greeted him mildly. "Mornin', Jack. Forgot to dust her off this time, didn't you?"

"No." Jack felt his voice wavering, but pushed on. "No, I didn't. I got sick of being called names by the rest of the gang, and cleaning for my ride after firing for my day's pay and all. It's just"—he heard himself finish in a contemptible bleat—"not fair at all."

Root smiled at him. "S'all right, Jack. I don't blame you. You're right. You fire and clean just like the other boys do, and I'll run just like the other runners do. No use in being odd."

Almost giggling with relief, Jack bent to his shovel, wondering if more things in life would come so easily if you were only man enough to demand them.

Root was chatty and affable as they pulled out of Duluth at 2 P.M. with the Number Four Limited—two chair cars, a smoker, a mail coach, a day car, and a baggage coach. Then, as soon as they cleared the station, he jammed the injector on full and McGowan had a hard half hour's work bringing his green fire up, with the pressure down twenty pounds. He was tired and sweaty by the time he'd finished, and just then the engine started churning water through the stack, plastering the front windows of the cab with dope. "Sorry, Jack," the engineer said amiably, "guess I forgot to shut off the injector. Must be getting old. Well, now we're rolling."

But Root was working her hard, and it told on the coal pile. Jack had to jump about twice as fast as usual. "This is an awful hard-pulling train," he said finally.

"Certainly is," said Root, and slapped the injector on again, treating Jack to another half hour of hot scrambling.

At last Jack said, "Jim, I think you're doing this on purpose."

Root looked puzzled. "Doing what?"

"Pounding this goddamned engine so hard and working water and pulling my fire all to hell. Why, I've shoveled sixty, seventy bushels of coal already."

"You know any other engine on this road that wouldn't have taken seventy bushels by now?"

"Naw, but this one never did before."

"Ah, 'before,' " said Root benignly. "Well, Jack, the way I look at it, before is when we were working together. Now you're working like the other firemen, and I'm running like the other drivers. You don't like it, you can piss up a string. Or you can clean the engine the way you used to, and I'll drive the way I used to." The water had slipped to one gauge again and Root put on the injector.

"Aw, hell, Jim, you win. I'll put a polish on her when we get in tonight, but gentle up on it now, will you?"

"Why, sure, Jack, if you prefer it that way." Root eased up a notch on the throttle and soon Jack had his fire back in order. He'd been so taken up with Root's goddamned object lesson that only then did he notice what was going on outside.

"Look there, Jim." They were pulling into Carlton, fifty-two miles north of Hinckley. "There's stumps burning along the track."

"Sure enough," said the engineer.

"And look at this smoke. You ever see it this bad before?"

"Jack, I've been driving through smoke for forty years. There's always more or less smoke, this time of year. Don't worry."

But it looked bad to McGowan, and he did worry.

The business with Jack cheered Root up.

His goddamn funny bone had hurt him so much he'd had to lift his coffee cup with his left hand that morning. He'd probably made a face, too, because Emily was so concerned she pretended not to notice, instead of pestering him to see the doctor again. She didn't say a word; just put his second cup down next to his left hand. He hadn't told her what the doctor had said, but she'd guessed somehow. That's what came from being married for a quarter century. No privacy.

The arm had loosened a little by the time he got to the yard and found his engine standing there with the crap from yesterday's running still pasted all over it, and McGowan sitting up in the cab like a sultan, taking in the day.

He'd almost shouted at Jack, but then he had another idea, and it had worked out fine and Jack would be tractable from now on. Jack was a good stoker and he would make a good engineer in time. Root had no children—that had pained him and Emily a lot, years ago—and it gave him real pleasure to take a sprout like Jack and make him into a railroadman. Root would get old, leave the road, die in a chair in his parlor, and Jack would get old too, but the trains would go on forever, it being America they were running in.

So Root, happy in the success of his roundabout tutoring, paid little attention to the burning stumps around Carlton. "There's always more or less smoke this time of year," he told Jack, who kept pulling at his brand-new moustache and looking unhappy.

South of Carlton it got dark. The train jogged along and Root leaned back and forth with the motion, left hand lolling on the throttle, acting as if it were the same as any other run, while the reformed Jack kept busy with the firebox.

Finally, though, Root couldn't see the water glass. "Better light the cab lamp," he told Jack in an offhand way, as if this were standard procedure on any summer run when four o'clock rolled around.

The fireman wasn't fooled. "What about this, Jim?" he wanted to know.

"I've never seen it like this before, Jack, and that's the truth. But there's no fire. Do you see any fire?"

"No, but it's black as the inside of a dog."

Root looked out his window. He couldn't see the trees, just flat black smoky shapes that seemed to revolve slowly as he stared at them. For a moment he had the feeling that the train wasn't moving at all, that it was standing stock still, vibrating in the dark. Then some sparks from the stack whipped back past the window and showed Root he was cutting right along.

"Better light the head lamp, too," he said.

They lit it at Barnum, where more than the usual crowd of depot loafers stood staring up at the locomotive, as though Root might have something to tell them.

Sullivan, the conductor, came into the cab. "Lamps are on in the cars," he said; "passengers seem edgy."

Sullivan seemed pretty edgy himself, scraping his foot on the deck and bending over to pick at a tear in Root's seat cushion. The station agent came out to say he couldn't raise Hinckley on the key. Then he stood peering up at the cab with the others, all their faces oddly pale and fragile under the slow roil of the sky.

With one convulsive pluck, Sullivan tore Root's cushion half open. "Sorry, Jim," he said. He rubbed his hands on his legs. "Maybe we should put her in the hole and wait here until we get some news from Hinckley. What do you think?"

Root had never felt especially cordial toward Sullivan. The man did his job, but he was always too high and mighty about it.

Conductors gave the law to engineers, but any conductor worth his salt occasionally deferred to the engineer's knowledge. Sullivan never did, and he never joked with the crew after the run. And when he came up into the cab, he always acted as if he were afraid of getting his suit dirty. This was the first time he'd ever asked Root what he thought.

"I think it's my job to put the train through, unless I'm told otherwise. Nobody's told me otherwise. You want to lay out, I'll lay out. But it's your say-so, not mine."

McGowan lifted his head, started to say something, changed his mind. Root knew he wanted to lay out, too, but the boy kept quiet. He'd learned his lesson. Good stuff in Jack.

Sullivan fidgeted with his watch. "Might be some fire up ahead."

"Then folks'll be waiting for the train, won't they?"

Sullivan gave Root a venomous smile. "Jim," he said, which was the first time Root had heard the man call him by his Christian name, "maybe we ought to talk it over, decide together."

The engine spluttered and popped. Jack had a good deal of steam up.

"I'm waiting for orders," Root said.

Sullivan climbed down from the cab. "Ah, hell. Take her out." Root whistled, opened the throttle, and looked back as Barnum slid away. The station loafers watched him go. Standing grave and separate, they might have been the last people left alive on earth. Root kept looking back at their small white faces until Jack asked him what he was doing.

They ran through darkness for about thirty miles. McGowan grumbled and worried, but didn't see any fire. There was plenty of smoke, though; it moved thick and heavy through the cab, and drawing a breath was like sucking through a straw.

Root kept his eye on the gauges. His arm was hurting him again.

As they rounded the bend just past Miller Junction, calm yellow light bloomed all around them. Root saw it first on the boiler—a flat, steady glow that showed up every seam and rivet but cast no shadows.

"Jesus Christ," said McGowan, "look!" Root saw dozens—scores—of people running his way. "There must be something wrong in

Hinckley," he heard himself say.

A woman in front of the crowd reached the barbed wire fence that the railroad had strung to keep livestock off the tracks. She jumped clear over it, then turned and pulled a little boy across. Root saw the barbs cut long gouges in his bare legs. Then everyone was at the fence. A man in a green coat fought briefly with a tall woman for possession of a foot of it, then punched her in the face. She grabbed her chin and fell back into the crowd, and he got over ahead of her.

"What the hell's the matter?" squeaked Jack.

There was nothing behind the people but that bland, butterscotch light.

"Something must—" Root stopped with his jaw so wide open he felt his tongue vibrating, but couldn't close his mouth. A mountain of flame taller than any building he'd ever seen drew all the yellow light into it. Smooth and solid as custard, the color of blood and lemons and egg yolk, it rolled toward the train.

Jack made an intense, tiny noise: "Eeeee. Eeeeee."

Root could feel it coming, not from the heat it had to be throwing out, but in a vibration in the deck of the cab, multed and strong and on the edge of sound, like the distant flow of summer thunder.

It was maybe a quarter mile behind the desperate people at the fence, with a narrow stand of trees between it and them. It walked over the trees, and they bent down limply and just disappeared.

Root saw Sullivan run out to the fence and stand there jumping like a snap toy while John Monihan, the brakeman, helped people across and pushed them toward the train. The fire welded a sharp black shadow to everyone: thin lines with bulges on the ends jittered across the sides of the cars as the people ran for them.

The flame pulled up the soil in slender, turning spouts. The spouts burned like sparklers, zigzagging along ahead of the tough, bulging hide of the fire.

I've got to close my mouth, Root thought. He worked the right muscles, and his mouth closed. Now I've got to think. He had no thoughts. He looked at the valves and levers on the back head, the tools he had used for forty years. They might have been a page of Chinese poetry, for all they meant to him now.

The fire picked up a stake wagon, bore it gently and slowly into the sky until the wood disappeared and the iron dropped away.

I've got to think.

But Jack was still screaming his field-mouse scream, the fire was eating up the earth, and the controls still looked like a pile of old hoes and rakes in the corner of a barn. Root simply couldn't connect them with the possibility of escape; there was no getting away from that limitless flame. He was sitting in an iron room. He might as well be sitting in a corncrib watching death boil toward him across a field.

A woman appeared at the gangway. Her eyebrows had burned away, leaving her face looking smooth and young. "For God's sake," she screamed, "will you save us?"

Behind her, Sullivan called, "Everybody's on. Jesus, Jim, get us out of here."

Root looked at the back head, and the alien iron turned back into the controls. He took hold of the Johnson bar, threw her into reverse—his arm didn't give so much as a twinge—took hold of the throttle, and then had to make himself think again. Where to go?

He remembered running through the darkness a few minutes earlier, seeing the yellow square of light from his cab window passing over water: Skunk Lake. A scummy, brackish little pond—a puddle more than a lake—six miles back.

"I'm going for Skunk Lake," he told Jack; "move dirt."

Jack stopped bleating and picked up his shovel.

"Look after the end of the train," Root called to Sullivan. "I'm going back to Skunk Lake."

The conductor actually wrung his hands, rubbed them together as though he were washing them. Root had never seen anybody do that before. "We'll never get there alive."

"Then we'll all die together," Root called jauntily. All the symptoms of physical fear had taken him—his hair felt like hot wires in his scalp, his hands were cold and prickly—but he was still elated at having remembered how to run his engine.

He cracked the throttle and the Number Four Limited started backing away from Hinckley.

Root hadn't gone more than thirty feet when the fire bellied toward him, slamming into the train and driving the better part of the cab window glass into his face and neck.

Keegan had sat waiting to die with his mind as close to empty as it had ever been, and so he turned a child's eyes on the locomotive when it appeared; saw it as big, miraculous, and perfect with the blithe movement of its connecting rods. And then the buttery light shone down on it and made it all the more wonderful.

He rose to his feet without effort, ran easily across the field, and floated over the barbed wire fence at its boundary. The thump and whoosh of the fire behind him brought back the crowded terror of the past two hours, but the train remained perfect as he ran toward it. It was going to save his life.

Everyone else was aboard already, and Keegan faltered for a second. He hurt all over. He couldn't cover the last fifty feet. The train would leave and he'd die after all.

There. The train started backing, the engine throwing short, scornful bursts of steam out of its cylinders. Keegan jumped for a car, grabbed the handhold, and saw a big black hand close over his wrist. A porter in a clean blue uniform pulled him into the vestibule and regarded him with pink eyes. "There, sir," he said calmly, "all aboard."

Keegan, choking down painful swallows of air, felt at once mortally ill and terrifically light-headed and clear of vision. The iron openwork along the vestibule railing was beautiful. The curved spokes of the brake wheel were beautiful. He rubbed his face; it was smooth and moist. "Is—" He coughed, spat. "Is my hair all gone?"

"No, sir," said the porter, "just in the front."

Keegan swayed and stumbled with the motion of the train. The porter took him by the elbow and steadied him. "Thank you."

"You're welcome, sir. I'm the porter, John Blair. Best step inside now, sir."

Keegan stumbled again, but Blair kept him on his feet and steered him into the car. Keegan saw a long, smoky gallery, crowded with people, all of them standing transfixed, staring out of the left-hand windows, their eyes full of bloody light.

Keegan saw it all: the brilliant dust on the seat cushions, the car lamps swaying, patches of dirty skin showing through torn clothes, and Betty, staring out the windows with the others, her face, all the faces, tense and vacant.

Just then Keegan's mind was a photographic plate; his thoughts barely moved behind the images. Before he could wonder what they were all looking at, the fire came thundering up against the car.

It came like thunder. It came like wind. Yellow flame blew through the car and swallowed up the screaming in a scalding rush of noise. The air was full of flying glass. The flame passed, leaving the seats burning behind it.

Keegan was still on his feet. A slow thought came to him: all the windows are broken. No. The nearest one had ballooned inward and still hung in its frame, carrying radiant reflections on its soap-bubble surface. As Keegan looked at it; it burst into powder.

"It melted," he said aloud. "By God, it melted." And with that he had his mind back. The train was still moving. People were getting up from the floor of the car. They were all pretty quiet except for one woman who sat bolt upright in her seat, screaming, with her hair burning. Keegan took a step toward her, but Blair was there first. Wrapping a wet towel around her head, he said, "There, that'll do now, ma'am. I'll just fix you another one." He came up the aisle to Keegan. "Excuse me, sir, but could I trouble you to pass wet towels out from the lavatory? I expect we'll be needing them."

"Sure," said Keegan. "Just a minute."

He stepped around a hard-looking business type who had managed to keep his cigar intact through the explosion of fire and came up behind Betty. He touched her shoulder. "You all right?"

She turned, shrieked, and took his hands in hers. "Oh, you're here! I didn't see you. Where were you?"

"Right behind you. I'm fine."

"Good. Good."

"I'm going to get some towels for people. I think we're safe now."

Making his way to the lavatory, Keegan realized he didn't think anything of the sort. Thick black smoke rolled past the windows, and thought the seat fires had been extinguished, embers kept sleeting in to start more. People were recovering from the concussion and some had started shouting.

Keegan found a stack of towels above the sink, soaked one and handed it out to Blair, who nodded his thanks. The porter went down the aisle calling in the loud, confident voice he might have used to announce dinner being served in the dining car, "Please keep still, ladies and gentlemen. We'll be out of danger soon, if you'll just please keep still."

On Blair's fourth or fifth stop at the lavatory, Keegan told him, "I'm about out of towels. Bring some back and I'll wet them again."

"I'll surely do that."

Keegan stopped him as he turned away. "Say, just what do you think our chances are?"

The porter gave him a quick, judging glance. "About one in twenty thousand," he said, and strode off down the aisle calling, "Towels, wet towels coming through. Just keep calm and everything'll be dandy."

Keegan soaked the last of the towels and looked out into the aisle. The overhead lamps hung weak and gassy in the murk, but the detonations outside the windows were constant enough now to keep a glow playing up and down the car. Stained with foundry light, passengers surged this way and that, trying to keep inside shifting pools of cooler air.

A few seats away, Keegan saw a little boy yanking at his father's sleeve, crying, "Do we have to die, Papa? Papa, do we have to die?" The father bent toward him and spoke. Keegan couldn't hear his reply but he could see a natural-born salesman at work; the man calmed the child down in seconds. But just then a huge, chunky, badly formed man, a stack of stones left over from when there were giants in the earth, came barreling through the car keening, "We're all going to die, we're all going to the Lordy. Lordy, Lordy, we're all going to die. Oh, flee from the wrath to come, we're going to the Lordy."

Keegan ducked back into the lavatory as the fanatic went flailing past into the next car. The man left the boy crying again in his wake, and when Keegan came out with more towels for Blair he saw Betty kneeling in the aisle, comforting the child. Were it not for her bare, bruised legs, she would have looked just like a schoolmarm. The car was filled with such placid incongruities: down the aisle a wispy young man rose to offer his seat to a bleeding matron. A little girl, plaiting her doll's hair—Keegan supposed that was what little girls did with their dolls' hair—sat in the lap of her unconscious mother. The woman's face was black with smoke, and the man next to her kept dabbing her forehead with one of Blair's towels. The man's mouth was set in a weeping grin but, when the little girl turned around to see what was going on, he opened it into a good parody of a real grin. Reassured, she returned to her doll, he to his terrified smirk. Blair came up the aisle and patted the child on her head. "That your dolly? What's her name? He reached behind the girl's head, deftly twitched the towel out of the man's hand, and replaced it with a freshly moistened one. "Penelope!" he boomed. "That's some big handle for a little doll." He laughed. Everyone was safe as houses. He moved on.

When Keegan took the bundle of dried towels from Blair, sparks dripped out of it. "Sorry, sir," said the porter, "kind of hard to keep track of things today."

Keegan dumped the towels in the sink, but before he could wet them pelting embers dissolved the frosted glass of the lavatory window. For a moment the small room was filled with hot, blunt shrapnel.

Keegan kept his eyes shut until things stopped stinging him. When he could finally look again, he saw Blair holding his face. "You all right?"

The porter bucked his head up out of his hands. "Course I am. What—"

"Toadstools." Keegan had seen the floor where the fifty-odd wind-driven mushrooms that had blown in the window were still burning. The two men stamped them out.

"Mushrooms came in like bullets," said Blair. "This some kind of day."

"Your face is cut." Keegan mopped off the blood, black on Blair's forehead, red on the towel.

"I got my hat?"

"Right on your head."

Blair straightened his hat until it was at its most official angle. "Those towels ready?"

"Hell. Sorry." Keegan wet the towels quickly and handed them to the porter.

"Wet towels coming," Blair shouted into the aisle, but before he could leave the lavatory the train lurched and slowed so suddenly that the porter was thrown up against the doorjamb.

"What're we stopping for?" Keegan asked.

"Engineer knows what he's doing," Blair said hastily and carried the towels into the aisle. Keegan followed him out. He thought the train had stopped, but then he saw a single burning tree. It stayed framed in the nearest window for a long, long time, but at last it moved away.

The ceiling of the car had caught fire. Wet towels couldn't do a thing about that. Melting paint dripped on people's heads. Everybody was screaming. The train stopped.

Root didn't know the cab window glass had cut him until a second explosion filled the cab with orange light, and he saw, out of the corner of his eye, dark spray jetting from somewhere under his chin. He pulled a glove partway off, touched the back of his wrist to his neck, and held it to the cab lamp; it was covered with blood.

"How bad'm I cut?" he asked Jack, but the fireman didn't hear him. He was pointing at something on the tracks ahead of the backing locomotive. Root forgot about the cut, stuck his head out of the cab window, and saw three men chasing the engine. They were only a few yards away, leaping over the burning ties. Root reached for the brake. Jack pushed his hand away.

"What the hell—" Root stopped himself. Jack was right. The ties had to be afire for miles on either end of the train. If he stopped, the air hoses would burn away, the brakes would lock, and they'd roast where they sat. He took the throttle instead, opened it a notch, and turned his head away from the desperate men. Jack was trembling so much that he could barely get his shovel through the firebox door.

When Root looked again, two of the men were gone, but the third had jumped and made it. He clung to the cowcatcher, a big, fierce-looking man with a single eye beaming wrath out of a murderer's face. Root waved to him. "Hang on!" The man couldn't have heard him, didn't need the advice anyway.

Root turned to check on Jack. His neck felt wet and slick as though he was wearing a fine silk scarf. His mother had had a real silk scarf; she'd let him handle it when he was little. It had moved through his hands like water.

Jack was doing fine, crouched down, swiveling between tender and firebox like a figure on a penny bank. Good boy. Make a real good runner one day. Root smiled at Jack. Have to bring him home, show him to the wife. Just like having a son.

The man on the cowcatcher was doing fine, too. Root smiled at him. Poor one-eyed bastard, he was having a hard ride of it. The fire billowed gently around the engine. Pretty good fire. Sometimes it went away and then Root was sleepy, but when it came back it kept him awake, it rolled and spurted so. Came up to the side of the train and went away like the ocean. Root had seen the ocean twice, and this fire was just as interesting. The ocean had white crisscrosses on it when it came in, and the fire had dark crisscrosses.

The fire ebbed back into the woods and it was dark for a long time. Jack kept moving, dim in the cab light, wide awake. Smoke curled past him like sleep, and sparks glided by. They pulsed and died like fireflies. Root thought of his mother's scarf, and slept.

Heat woke him. More heat then he'd felt all day, more heat then he'd felt in his life. The fire was tall outside, the cab bright and empty as a morning kitchen. "Jack!" No Jack.

Root blinked at the steam gauge. Only ninety-five pounds of pressure on the clock. The engine wasn't moving.

He yanked the throttle open—he'd apparently fallen forward and almost shut it.

"Jack!"

The engine jolted backwards, nearly threw him off his seat. Good. There wasn't a thing he could do about the steam gauge, with Jack gone, so he looked out the window. The fire was crashing through the forest, all harsh angles and sudden flares. Big trees bowed back horizontally, then snapped forward to catapult balls of fire into other trees. The sky had three lucent layers; fire flowed back past the train on the lowest and highest, forward in the middle. Root saw the middle layer drop a great shape of fire—an Indian club or a milk bottle—down through the lower one into the woods. It burst, and whole trees rose into the sky, dripping dirt from their roots.

"Jack!"

Root guessed he'd been asleep a mile or two. Skunk Lake couldn't be too far. The tracks were soft, the locomotive lolled this way and that as it backed. It was like running on jelly.

"Jack!" Root heard something, turned around—his neck didn't feel so good now—and saw McGowan climbing out of the manhole in the tender, his wet overalls sparkling. "Get the hell down here! Get down here now, you silly bastard!"

Jack came down as Root started to topple. The fireman stuck out an arm, and water dripped on Root's face like music. "My God, give me some more of that," he said, "go and draw a pail of water."

Root's hands hurt him. He pulled off his gloves and saw them, pale pink and swollen to twice their usual size. His fingers were fat as sausages.

Jack set down the pail and Root dipped his hands in it. "Yes. Oh, yes." He rubbed his hands together in the sweet, chilly water. A putty-colored fissure opened on his left palm. "I can't rub them," he told McGowan. "The skin'll come right off."

"There's blood all over you," said the fireman.

Root touched his neck. "I got cut." He hooked his elbow over the sill and forced his head around against his neck's hard, stiff hurting. Every car was on fire; the paint was already gone from their sides. The sky burned dark red and salmon overhead, but the woods were black. He had no idea where they were.

"Have we passed Skunk Lake?"

"Dunno," said Jack.

Root squinted up the tracks. His eyes stung terribly and he had to shake the tears from them every few seconds.

"You *should* know. If we passed it while you were hiding in the tank—"

"Well, you were asleep," Jack replied in an aggrieved soprano.

Root didn't answer. Skunk Lake was the last water for fifteen miles. If they'd passed it, that was that. They were all dead.

The sky darkened. All Root could see was the burning cars. They threw off enough light to show him the passengers boiling around inside, but the smoke from the forest was so thick that he couldn't make out anything along the right-of-way. It was like something he might have done in the war: pushing burning stuff across a high trestle at midnight.

"We've gone by it, Jim" McGowan said humbly. "I'm sorry."

Root turned from the window. "You sure?"

"I think so." McGowan put his hands over his eyes like a guilty child.

Root dropped a hand on his shoulder. "Hell, Jack, it's not your fault. We did our best."

McGowan nodded. The heat had already dried his clothes, and pressed them somehow. They had a hundred flat, shiny surfaces, and crackled as he bent to pick up his shovel.

Root checked the gauges. "How're we for coal?"

"Fine. It's water we're poor on. What do we do?"

"You shovel. I'll run us out of this."

McGowan threw coal. "You think we can get clear?"

"You bet," Root lied. "I've run through fires worse than this."

He'd never seen anything worse than this. Not at Andersonville, with its walking dead. Certainly not the smoke of other Minnesota summers. It did get bad sometimes, so bad he'd thought, What if it all goes up? But it never had.

The absolute blackness outside wouldn't be so scary, either, except it was late afternoon. Somewhere above that phony night was bright blue sky. The fire would come back soon, and it would take them. He'd seen how that fire could move.

He opened the throttle wide. No use worrying about the water now; there wasn't enough water in the world to get them out of this.

Well, he'd go out on the limited, not in some filthy little kettle of a yard engine.

"Keep at it, Jack. We'll be fine in a minute." No use alarming the boy.

He wondered if the one-eyed man was still on the pilot. Yes, hanging on. Did they have any cars left? He looked back down the train again. The cars were still there, still burning—and each car carried a burning twin beneath it.

They were over water.

Root big-holed her: grabbed the Johnson bar and threw the engine into forward with one hand while he closed the throttle with the other. He'd been ready for the jolt of the stopping train, but it knocked him to the deck anyway.

"Skunk Lake," he said. He tried to push himself up from the floor of the cab, but his hands hurt too much. Jack took hold of him. "Get up, Jim."

"Leave me alone. Go help the passengers off. Take water. They can't get down unless you throw water on the steps."

Jack kept pulling at him. "Come on! Get in the water!"

"You go *now*," said Root, and it was all he could do to put the stress on the "now." "I run the show here, and if you don't go, I'll have you back firing yard goats."

McGowan picked up the bucket and scrambled out of the cab. Root lay back on the deck, but it was too hot on his face, so he curled up, an arm between his cheek and the sizzling iron.

Gradually it got bright again. The fire was back. He hoped the passengers had all gotten out. He should get out too. But getting up and moving to the gangway would be so much work that the thought of it made him want to weep. He squirmed a little, then lay still.

The second stop threw Keegan against the wall of the lavatory and pitched Blair into his arms. The two men hung on to each other while the train crashed to a halt.

Somewhere along the way, Keegan had been taken by a sense of jaunty inconsequence. He knew the car was full of burned, bloody people, knew they were all careering along to ghastly extermination, knew he had to keep passing wet towels to Blair. But there was a cool, wry little spot in the back of his skull, and it gave him comfort.

He looked down into Blair's face and laughed. "Engineer still know what he's doing?"

Blair laughed too. That miffed Keegan for a moment. He wanted to be the only one strong enough to be amused. Then he remembered the day before when LeMoyne was braying out his forty-five minute coon joke, and Blair standing there gravely, ready to offer the fat man a match if he should happen to want a fresh cigar during his dialect. Maybe colored people had the cool, wry place all the time.

Blair disengaged himself. "Better check the car, sir."

Keegan followed him out and for a moment he thought everybody had died. Men and women lay heaped in the aisle. No, they were alive. They twitched and shouted and pushed themselves to their feet. Everyone was cut and black and dirty, except for their teeth. Keegan saw a lot of teeth; a lot of breasts, too. The women were making no effort to cover their nakedness. The men weren't noticing. Keegan was the only one who saw.

The paint on the roof had all melted. Now there was nothing but fire overhead, and fire shooting in through the windows.

Most of the seats were burning, and people pushed into the aisle, hitting each other with fists, stepping on wailing children.

"Now stop! Now just stop it!" Blair, stolid and loud enough to calm them all for a moment.

Halfway down the car, Keegan saw the flash of brass on a conductor's hat. The trainman held up a little girl. Keegan thought he was going to try to pass her forward. Cool types on the St. Paul & Duluth.

"Everybody's dead!" the conductor screamed. "Everybody's burned!" He lifted the child over his head, poised himself to pitch her through a window.

"Stop, Mr. Sullivan," Blair shouted, battering his way down the aisle.

"Everybody's dead!" The conductor threw the girl. Betty jumped in front him. Keegan saw a small black shoe graze her face, saw her seize the child by its legs, hold it dangling for a moment, then turn it upright and set it down.

And that was the last of the cool, wry place in his mind. He pushed toward Betty, got a glimpse of Blair holding the child, and then the planks of the roof began to spring, pelting everyone with sparks and molten nails.

Keegan screamed with the rest, covered his head with his arms, and tried to get to the end of the car. The crowd pushed him up against a stout woman clutching a carpet bag. She drew her lips back over her teeth. "Don't touch me. Don't you touch me." He reached for her shoulder to push her aside. She snapped at his hand.

The back of the chair beside him burst, pouring fire onto the seat. A lighting fixture swayed and fell. The woman didn't budge. Hands pushed at Keegan's back. "Keep away, you," the woman said in a low, furious voice. "I know what you want."

"I want to get the hell out of this car, lady." He was close to hitting her when a voice, louder than the rest, shouted, "Off! Everybody off! Get in the water!"

Water? Keegan looked over his shoulder and saw a grimy trainman at the end of the car holding a bucket. "That's right," Blair's deep, calm voice called from somewhere. "You all listen to Mr. McGowan. We're at Skunk Lake."

The pressure against Keegan eased as men and women tottered past the trainman and out of the car. Keegan left the stout woman for Blair to deal with as he chose, and walked up the aisle. He was tired again, could feel his legs trembling. On the last seat next to the door, he saw a plump gold watch, its chain wrapped around the arm of the chair. It never occurred to him to pick it up.

"Hurry, mister!" The trainman, a kid with a brand-new moustache, sloshed water from the bucket onto the steps. "Get off and into the lake."

"Thanks." Keegan glanced back down the length of the car. Every inch of woodwork was burning now, and flames fizzed from white-hot centers where the seats fed them.

"Hurry!"

"Sorry." Keegan jumped from the car, the trainman behind him. The wind immediately knocked him to his knees. He saw fire ahead; there wasn't any water. The fire moved, broke into shimmering spangles—it was the reflection from the burning cars. Keegan crawled forward, tumbled down a small embankment, and splashed into warm muck. On hands and knees, he hiked himself away from the embankment. Rank water rose to his elbows; something slimy and full of small bones squirmed out from under his hand.

The wind grew stronger as he crawled and blew spray in his face. He looked around for the others, but it was too dark to see them. He felt ooze squirting between his fingers, salving his hands. The water rose, thick and warm, to his neck. As he thrashed along, the broken surface picked up glints of light from the train.

A greater light came from behind, strong enough to turn the water milky around him, and to throw the shadow of his head on it. He turned to see a sheet of fire rising from the east. Torn and boiling along the top, it arced upward, driving incandescent scud before it. He ducked his head underwater as the flame smashed by above. He saw the redness of it through his closed eyes, and when he raised his head thunder was still trembling in its wake.

It left the sky a pale pink, which quickly began to fade. Keegan looked around. Hundreds of heads were lifting out of the water. People started to call out: "Charles! Charles!" "Mommy!" "Gretchen! I'm here, Gretchen!"

Keegan began shouting, too. "Betty! Betty!" She wasn't family, and he felt a little guilty adding to all those frantic voices, but he didn't want to be alone. "Betty!" She had to be nearby; he'd got off the car only seconds after she had. He half swam, half crawled past a man who was holding an infant and wiping its face with a handkerchief, and a very old woman who peered about her with a bright, empty smile.

"Betty!"

Keegan bobbed past the man who had so effectively calmed the boy on the train. He seemed about at the end of his rope. The boy squalled and shuddered while he said with desperate heartiness, ". . . and then we'll all get some ice cream."

"Betty!"

He heard her voice. "Who is that?"

"Me. Scott Keegan."

He heard splashing behind him and turned to see her, wide-eyed and trembling, black slashes of wet hair across her face.

"Hello." He reached out and took her hands. She let him hold them for a moment, then drew them away.

The eastern sky grew bright again; fire gathered itself there like sunrise. "Better get down," Keegan said.

"They're all in the swamp, Jim. Come along now." McGowan was back, had his hands under Root's arms, and someone was pulling at his feet. The conductor?

"Sullivan?"

"Nah," McGowan said, "Sullivan went off his head. They say he tried to throw a kid out the window."

"He dead?"

"Who knows." It was Monihan, the brakeman.

"Monihan, why aren't you helping—"

"Everybody's out but you, Jim. Stop pissing about it and come along."

They were lifting him out of the cab. He dabbed his feet gently at the rungs of the gangway ladder, trying to help, humiliated to think how many times he'd swung right from the cab to the ground on the grab iron, never once using the steps. He was getting to be an awful old lady.

They had him on his back; they had him in the water. He tried to raise his head to get a look at the engine; but before he could, fire banged through the sky. The explosion knocked him under the surface. Somebody—Jack or Monihan—kept an arm around his neck. He breathed water, was lifted, coughing and puking, to breathe searing air.

"That's two of those bastards," he heard Monihan say. "How many times is that goddamned fire going to come back?"

"It sure makes a noise," said McGowan. "It's—"

Root interrupted. "The engine."

"What?" McGowan was right next to him, chin-deep. The wind slapped the scummy water into small waves around them.

"The engine." The coal was burning in the tender; hard red bars of light ran forward through the cab windows along the boiler.

"Come on, Jack. We can save the engine. Get under her and cut the tender and I'll run her off."

"Jesus, Jim, leave it alone. Nothing can live up there."

Root had spent his life on the road. He moved in the water. It was only a couple of feet deep. He rolled on his belly and started crawling toward the train. The burning cars made the lake almost too bright to look at.

"I won't go, Jim."

"Come on, then, Monihan."

"Shit," the brakeman said. But in the end they both followed Root up the embankment, which steamed and crackled as their wet clothes touched it.

McGowan put a hand under Root's ass and shoved him into the cab. The lamp was still going, and it looked calm and familiar in there, even with the tender blazing.

Root checked the gauges—not much steam left. "Hurry up, Jack." McGowan gave a long, foul reply, but at last there was a scrape and a clank. "She's free, you crazy old bastard."

Root opened the throttle. At first he thought she didn't have the sap for it, but then he heard the steam shuddering lax into the cylinders, and Number Sixty-nine edged herself forward a yard, two yards, three yards—stopped.

It was enough.

Root reached for the grab iron, realized it would burn him to the bone. "Help me down, Jack."

"Yeah, sure, and then I want to wipe the goddamned jacket and black the goddamned stack, too."

It hurt his face some, but Root smiled as Jack and Monihan lowered him back into the swamp.

After the second wave of fire had passed, Betty lay in the warm silt next to Keegan, the stranger whose life she had saved, and who had saved her life.

Stumps were burning near and far, and, beyond the guttering cars, the fire was building for another colossal leap. Nevertheless, she had come this far; had come to a place where the fire couldn't get at her.

Her throat ached and her eyes stung, but she felt drowsy and languid. She knew that sooner or later she would have to go over the horrors of the long day. But right now her brain, kindly organ that it was, had them muted: dim, still little pictures.

Later she would have to find out if her parents had survived. And she would have to grieve for Tom Dunn. She thought of him at his key, ready to die a hero's death, paying off whatever debt he felt he owed since the night Sy Hornby got drunk and wrecked the limited. If the fire hadn't come, he would have sought out some other way to pay. It would have been no life with Tom. She let him go.

"Here it comes," Keegan said calmly. He put his hand on her shoulder and pushed her under the surface as the flame rumbled over. It was still strong enough for her to feel the concussion of its passing in the lake bed, but it wasn't as powerful as the other two had been.

Keegan helped her up and she shook water from her hair. All around her, people coughed and murmured and called out to each other: a great, muttering sound of life rising from the smoky swamp.

Something seemed to be wrong with her ears. She pressed on them, then realized what it was.

"The wind is gone," she said.

The cars had burned themselves out, but the flames from the tender rose straight and pointed in the quiet air. The black sky paled to gray, so that she could see her bare knees moving under the water. Soft ash started falling, a few flakes at first that sent ripples out from where they lighted, then thousands of them. For as far as she could see, ash dropped from pale acres of sky, drifting up against the black stumps like snow. People brushed it from their hair. She heard somebody laugh.

"You know," Keegan said in a quiet, rusty voice, "before my famous success in the barber supply business, I sold books door to door. One season I had a big leather book of Dante's *Inferno*. It really was the size of a barn door. Anyway, some Frenchman had done drawings for it. And one of them showed what happened to you if you did a particular awfulness, I forget what. You got sunk in ice to your neck, and it snowed on you. And the picture looked just like this."

He opened his hand toward the people bobbing around in the gray water, under the gray fall of ash.

Frank Stone was about to knock off and go home when word came in that the wires were cut north of Pine City. It had happened before, but not too often, so he hung around the office until seven, drinking coffee and teasing the woman typewriter—a callous item who called him "sonny boy." The wires still weren't fixed, so he went to his boss, Mr. Fenner, and asked him for travel money.

Mr. Fenner was very funny. He offered Frank a nickel. "Sure. Take a streetcar home."

Stone laughed—keeping his job on the St. Paul Globe mostly involved pretending to enjoy a joke at his own expense. After a studied self-recovery he said, "The lines are down and I thought if I went up to Pine City tonight there might be something doing."

"Always something doing in Pine City." Mr. Fenner winked when he said "doing" and stuck his tongue out of the corner of his mouth. That would have been funny, or at least, comprehensible, if Pine City had an reputation at all as a whorehouse town. It hadn't.

"You want to get in on Pine City doings, spend your own money."

Stone laughed. He'd wanted to break Mr. Fenner's nose for three months now, but he had a new wife, a kitchen that needed curtains, and a baby on the way.

"I thought if I could catch the seven-thirty, I could find out what's happening. There's been talk of forest fires."

"Talk." Mr. Fenner looked wise and weary. "Gretchel never asked for traveling expenses because of talk. He just went out. Not that I'm telling you to go out. If there were any kind of fires, we'd know."

Hank Gretchel was the only reporter Stone had ever known who'd actually solved a murder. He'd done it a year ago; papers all across the country had picked it up, and twenty minutes later he'd gone east to work for Pulitzer on the World.

"Thank you, Mr. Fenner."

It was 7:20, so Stone wouldn't be able to tell his wife he'd be home late. She wouldn't mind that—she'd married a reporter, after all—but she'd sure be sore if he spent $1.85 going to Pine City for no good reason.

He worried on the train, and walked up and down the cars looking for a human-interest story. There wasn't one. No wan mothers alone with babies, no theater people, not even a traveling pet. And when, in desperation, he asked the conductor if anything interesting had happened lately, the man replied, "Nothing interesting ever happened to me in my whole life."

Stone gave up, went back to his seat, and watched people reading newspapers in the dull, homey car. He was famished, but when the candy butcher came through, he couldn't bring himself to part with a nickel for a candy bar.

It might have been election night in Pine City. The town smelled like spent firecrackers, and knots of people chattered away at each other under every streetlight. There was a regular crowd in front of the express office, and a lot of women were walking around crying.

Stone cheered right up.

" 'Scuse me, sir," he said to the first well-dressed man he saw. Rich folk always wanted to talk. "Has there been a fire?"

The man stopped, puffed himself up, and began to talk. You could count on it. "Indeed there has. Hinckley is destroyed, and the word is out that Mission Creek and Pokegama are gone too, and—"

"Were you in it?"

"No, but I know—"

"Who was?"

The man stopped, obviously annoyed. He pointed to a group of people near the depot.

"They're talking with some poor fellow who—"

"Thanks." Stone ran across the street to a bunch of thickly packed backs. He was a shy man normally, would walk a half mile to buy a sack of sugar rather than ask a neighbor for a tablespoonful. But newspapering wasn't like regular life. He shouldered his way into the crowd shouting, "Make way! Make way for the *Globe*!"

People made way. He punched his way through to a thin, blistered man sitting on a baggage cart.

"Hello, friend. You had some trouble? I'm from the *Globe*."

The man looked up at him and started to move his mouth slowly, as though he had to think about which muscles to use.

Ten minutes later, Stone went into the depot and tapped the busy telegrapher on the shoulder.

"I'm from the *Globe*. May I use the key?"

"Hell, no. Use the one at the hotel. This here's the railroad key."

"Hotel'll be full of people and they'll all want the key. What's your name?"

"Stanley Orro. Why?"

"Good. Mr. Orro, give me two minutes on this key and I'll put you in the paper. The sooner I get this news out, the sooner St. Paul will be sending aid. And you'll have something to show your folks—'Stanley Orro—the ordeal of a heroic telegrapher.' "

"Shit," said Orro, grinning. "You know how to use a key?"

Stone stuck out his arm and, standing, moving only the tips of his fingers, sent:

TO FENNER, GLOBE, ST. PAUL. HINCKLEY BURNED TO ASHES; MANY PEOPLE LOST THEIR LIVES IN THE FIRE, BALANCE ARE HOMELESS AND DESTITUTE: SEND RELIEF IF POSSIBLE AT ONCE. THE LITTLE TOWN OF MISSION CREEK ENTIRELY WIPED OUT. ENGINEER JIM ROOT PROBABLY FATALLY BURNED. SITUATION APPALLING AND HEARTRENDERING IN THE EXTREME.

STONE

"Damn, but you can handle that thing," said Orro. The sounder started. Orro answered. "Be a long one tonight," he told Stone, "track crews out all up and down the line, everything balled up."

Stone nodded, smiled. He was so happy Fenner hadn't given him the travel money. The bastard would have claimed he'd thought up the assignment himself.

"They're making up a relief train," Orro said, "if you're interested."

"You bet I am."

"It might be hard to get abroad. It'll be pretty tight."

"I got your key, didn't I? Tell me where it's making up. And keep an eye out for your name in the *Globe*."

Jemmy Stockholm walked through the streets of Duluth looking at all the brick buildings, the baby twitching in his arms. He had been to the city twice with his parents, but the buildings still surprised him. There weren't any brick buildings in Hinckley except the roundhouse and the new school, and they were probably gone now, along with his house. He thought of his house, and felt pressure at the top of his eyes, but no tears came. He'd cried himself out hours ago.

He had started crying soon after the man had pulled him into the freight car. He kept quiet about it, though, and nobody had noticed. Besides, other people were crying too, and it was dark and very hot.

Not long after they'd started, the train slowed and then the whole car lurched and sagged. Lots of people cursed, and a man opened the door a crack and there was some kind of post burning right outside.

"Christ, we're on a bridge!" He slammed the door shut. The train inched along. Jemmy, close to the floor of the car, could hear the wheels slowly turning. The train shuddered and swayed, and then picked up speed.

"God be praised," said a woman with a clear, sweet voice. She began to sing "Rock of Ages."

A few miles farther on, the air freshened a little. The car door opened again and a slice of real daylight—not the flat, moving fire glare—fell across Jemmy's lap. The baby stirred and mewed, but seemed to be holding up very nicely.

They traveled for hours; Jemmy's legs began to ache, and his wrist smarted where something had burned it. His throat was so dry that he could feel his breath scraping it raw. Swallowing was like trying to swallow a pebble.

The car quieted down. He kept his face away from the light so people couldn't see his tears had started up again. He wished his mouth were as wet as his eyes. He wondered where his parents were, and every time he closed his eyes he could see the dining room table sinking into the embers. He knew that people were dead; he'd seen dead people; but his mother and father couldn't be dead.

He thought about seeing the dead people, and wondered why it wasn't as terrible to him as certain stories he'd read in dime novels. Sometimes it was worse imaging things than actually seeing them. But he couldn't stop crying.

He must have slept some, because he woke up thinking he was home in the kitchen when the car door grated open and Duluth was outside.

He'd never seen so many people. They were all milling around and calling out from the platform, and behind them were ambulances and wagons.

He watched the crowd for a second from the car door, caught a glimpse of the tall buildings beyond, and then somebody set him down among all the legs. He pushed his way through, looking for his parents, but there were hundreds and hundreds of people.

"Mommy! Daddy!" Nobody paid any attention. He saw a man being carried past with a cloth over his face, and an old couple embracing, and then caught a glimpse of Winton Reese walking past with some kind of silly round college cap on his head, crying. Jemmy started after him, but lost him in the crowd. People kept jostling him, and he was scared they'd hurt the baby. He stopped and stood still, holding the infant and shuddering.

"Hey. Hey, sonny." A man crouched down in front of him. He smelled like cigars and looked as if he smiled a lot, but he wasn't smiling now. "Lose your folks?"

Jemmy nodded.

"Where? Here on the platform?"

"No. Back at home."

"Where's that?"

"Hinckley."

"Oh." The man wrinkled up his nose, then grinned. "Well, it's going to be a hell of a job finding them here just now. Tell you what, they're taking the injured to the Elks' Hall. You can go there, get your bearings, and then they'll find your mommy for you."

"But I'm not hurt."

"Bet you're thirsty, though."

Jemmy nodded. The man took the baby away from him.

"Hey!"

"Take it easy. I'll give him back. Last thing I want is a baby."

He led Jemmy through the crowd. "Is it a boy or a girl?" he asked when they'd gotten to the street.

Jemmy started to say he didn't know, then realized that that would sound pretty stupid and, if they thought it wasn't part of his family, they'd take it off somewhere. He couldn't have said why he wanted to keep the baby, but he did.

"It's a boy. My brother. His name is Billy." Everyone else's baby brother was named Billy. It seemed safe.

The man took him up a steep street—all Duluth was steep streets—into a brick building, up a flight of stairs, and into a room with dusty elk heads drooping from the walls. Cots were being set up, and the hall was full of people whose clothes smelled of smoke.

A nurse came over. The man whispered to her and handed her the baby. She smiled at Jemmy. "You must be exhausted. Here, come lie down."

"I'm fine," said Jemmy. "I want the baby back."

"Good luck, bub." The man tousled Jemmy's hair and trotted down the stairs before he could thank him.

The nurse led him to a bed. "I'll bring your brother right back as soon as I've changed him." Jemmy lay down. Smoky people walked back and forth, talking quietly with each other. A woman lay sobbing on a cot nearby. A bald man with gold spectacles on a black satin ribbon came by and wrote down Jemmy's name and his parents' names. The nurse returned with the baby and set the child down beside him. It was a boy. He'd guessed right. Jemmy fell asleep.

When he woke he thought the fire was back. But it was only night, which had come down outside the windows, and the blue gas jets that lit the room. A woman was taking the baby.

"Stop!"

She smiled at him. "I'm not stealing him." She pulled aside a dirty shawl—she'd been in the fire, too—and stuck a shiny brown nipple in the baby's face, right there in front of Jemmy.

"I'm sorry," he said, careful to look only in her eyes, the breast white at the edge of his vision.

"He was hungry," she said. "Oh my, he was hungry."

The baby went to sleep as soon as he had been fed, but Jemmy was wide awake now. He walked up and down the hall, looking in every bed. His parents weren't there.

The nurse came over, looking tired. "I have to go find my parents," he told her.

"They're checking. We'll know where they are in the morning."

"I want to go now."

"You can't find your way around in the dark."

"I can too," he lied. "I've been to Duluth lots of times."

"Nurse!" a man with a bloody face called.

She gave him a harried look, then told Jemmy, "Look in the Methodist church, right down the street."

"Thank you, ma'am."

Jemmy found the church without any trouble. As he walked up the steps he heard moaning inside, and a fat man in a derby stopped him at the door. "What do you want?"

"My parents. I'm from Hinckley."

"Oh, Christ," the man said in a sad voice. "What's their names?" Jemmy told him. He checked a list, shook his head. "Sorry."

"Where else should I look?"

"Well, they're taking 'em in at the Presbyterian church over on— but wait, try the depot first. They got 'em down there, too, and it's closer."

"Thank you."

"Good luck, kid." The man poked the baby's stomach. "Good-looking little sister you got there."

"It's my brother," said Jemmy.

He walked down to the depot, looking at all the brick buildings. One of them had a restaurant on the ground floor where men and women were eating chicken in a pink room while waiters in long aprons carried bottles around. Everyone looked very happy. There were an awful lot of streetlights, and Jemmy found the depot in about ten minutes.

He asked a man with an official-looking hat if his parents were inside. "I don't have a list, kid. Take a look. They've been coming in all night."

The dim room was full of people, some sleeping on the floor, some sitting up while doctors examined them. Near the door lay a man with no face.

They weren't in the waiting room, but Jemmy saw more people in the baggage room, sitting under kerosene lanterns. The air was thick there, and the baby started squirming.

Jemmy looked around. Under a lamp at the far end of the room he saw a little girl. His sister.

He opened his mouth, but had no voice. He ran forward, bumping against people, nearly stumbling. His father was sitting on a trunk with an arm around his mother.

"Muh—muh . . ." Her eyes opened wide. His father started to stand up. He talked fast; he knew he'd be crying soon. "A man gave me a baby. It's a boy. I think his mother is dead and—"

"Jemmy! Oh, Jemmy!" His mother took the baby.

"—And I said I'd look after it. And I did."

His father was staring down at him, a strange, angry little smile on his face. "It's nice you brought us another boy. Maybe he'll be better at stacking up the firewood and—"

Then he had his arms around Jemmy, and was sobbing big, horrible grown-up sobs.

September 2

"Look out! Easy! You're losing it! Stop the pissing vaudeville and move those goddamn cans."

"Come up and move them yourself, you horse turd!"

Under the spitting blue glare of a calcium lamp, three men were handling milk cans from the bed of a wagon onto a flatcar, while a fourth stood by, noisily dissatisfied with their progress. The cans made leaden gonging noises as they struck each other. Their hundred shallow dents ran with blue light.

Stone watched for a minute, then scribbled "pissing vaudeville" in his notebook, amused at the idea of trying to slip that vignette past his editor.

A coach stood behind the flatcar, its windows throwing wedges of light on the ground beside it. Stone walked back past it to another flatcar where men were loading raw lumber. A large man in a derby was directing them.

"I'm Frank Stone, from the *Globe*."

The man nodded. "Morning. Frank Webber."

Stone wrote in his book. "One *b* or two?"

"Two."

"That wood for new houses or some kind of track work?"

"Coffins."

"Coffins! Good God, how many do you expect to be burying?"

"They say maybe a hundred. Maybe more."

Stone whistled, then crossed out "pissing vaudeville." He probably wasn't going to be doing much joking about this.

"Who are you? I mean, to be doing this."

"I do undertaking for Mr. Cowan. He's the coroner. But I never had any business this big before. I don't think anybody did."

"Mind if I ride out with you?"

"I don't mind, but it isn't up to me. There'll be a lot of doctors and such going. I shouldn't think anybody'd mind."

Dawn was coming on thin and smoky when the train finally got under way. Stone had been sitting in the coach for three hours, dozing when the loading wasn't too noisy. The whistle woke him; he heard the trainmen croaking their incomprehensible jargon to each other, and then the car jolted forward.

"Good," said Stone to the wan young doctor who shared the seat with him.

"I don't know," said the doctor. "I never looked forward to a job less. Burns are horrible. Skin comes right off in your hands. And people always seem to be conscious."

"Bad, huh?" Stone wrote, "As a single dewdrop holds on its trembling surface the vast world around it, so was the scope of the tragedy contained in the gaunt and apprehensive features of one of the Pine City physicians who rallied in the dread watches of the night of September 1-2 to try to fan the spark of life from the embers of destruction. . . ." The sentence got away from him. He was very tired.

A mile outside of Pine City, the trees stopped. Stone had been this route a dozen times before, and the sudden brightening in the car startled him into full wakefulness. He looked out the window. The forest was gone. Stubbled with black stumps, the land ran flat and dreary to where low, dirty fires still burned a mile away.

"Look at that!" said Stone.

The doctor closed his eyes. "I know what's coming. I know."

The engine whistled and the slow train went slower still. "That'll be Mission Creek," someone said sitting behind Stone, then: "Christ, there's nothing there."

"Never was much," one of the gravediggers sang out jovially. "You want to lose a town, Mission Creek's the one to choose. I went there once and tried to—"

"Shut your coarse mouth," said Webber.

"Well, I *beg* your pardon," the man said in a surprisingly good attempt at a patrician St. Paul accent. "I merely hoped to divert my compatriots—"

"You're paid to dig, not to make a mockery of tragedy. You can walk back now if you don't want the job."

The gravedigger snorted, but shut up.

The four streets of Mission Creek laid a small gray grid over low humps of char. Near his window a trickle of gold flashed at Stone: the brass parts of the depot telegraph.

Stone started to write, "The dismal aspect . . ." but decided that was nowhere near strong enough and changed it to "Here were the fires of hell, burned out."

The train stopped and a battered-looking conductor with his jacket unbuttoned came into the coach. "Any reason to wait here?"

The doctors glanced at each other, then at Webber. He shook his head. "Nothing to bury."

"Nothing living out there, either," said the doctor next to Stone. "Better push on to Hinckley."

The conductor left, and a moment later the train started up again. Just past Mission Creek, the old post road curved in toward the track and ran along beside it for a couple of hundred yards. The fire had caught a wagon there and left it looking like four or five loops of barbed wire. Next to it lay a horse with its legs burned away to jagged stumps above the fetlocks. The animal had burst in the heat and spilled a thick satchel of guts onto the road.

"Damn," said the gravedigger who had annoyed Webber, "we're going to see *people* like that."

The undertaker turned and glowered, but there was no levity in the man this time.

For a half hour the train ground forward through blasted countryside while ash drifted down the aisle and everybody in the coach coughed. Then the locomotive groaned to a halt and the conductor appeared again.

"Head-of-track."

"Hey," said the vocal gravedigger, "this hasn't been head-of-track for thirty-five years."

"Head-of-track," the conductor repeated. "Beyond here, the rails are melted."

Stone stepped down into a pile of ash. His foot dropped through it and jarred against the ground; it was like stepping through the fine snow of early winter.

"How far is Hinckley?" he asked the doctor, who was already off and standing ankle-deep in ash.

"This is Hinckley."

"No." Stone looked around. "Hinckley's big. I've been through it."

The doctor opened his bag and checked the contents. "Should have brought more laudanum. Should've brought nothing but laudanum." He looked up at Stone. "It's Hinckley, all right. See, there's the roadhouse."

Stone saw what looked like a low stone wall. He couldn't tell how far away it was; there was no tree, no building, to help fix its position. Up ahead the locomotive, solid and comforting with its pipes and rivets and bulk, busily spilled steam and smoke into the steamy, smoky day.

"And the town?"

"Right there."

A water tower still stood, monumental in its solitude. Beyond it, fields of rubble sloped this way and that, some gray, some black. Here and there oily spars stuck up, but none rose more than a yard from the ground. A thousand cracks pumped spouts of dark smoke, as though a whole factory town were working under the crust of destruction.

"What—" Stone breathed in something harsh, coughed phlegm into his hand. "Excuse me. What will you do with the laudanum? Can anyone be left?"

"Well, there's someone."

Two ash-colored figures were picking their way toward them across the rubble. The doctor ran to them, Stone following. The ground was almost too hot to walk on and he bounced from foot to foot as he spoke with the survivors.

The larger man did the talking, red eyes wet in his gray face. "You a doctor? Good. This is Father Lawler. He's a little out of his head." The priest had his hands over his face. He muttered something about cheese.

"Will you take a look at him? He saved a bunch of people."

While the doctor examined Lawler, the other man said to Stone, "I'm Henly, section boss for the St. Paul and Duluth. It did come on. You never saw the beat of it. It got everything."

"How many people killed?"

"I don't know. I think most of 'em got out on the train. But there's about a hundred saved in the gravel pit. That's how I got through it. These other doctors too?"

Half a dozen men had come over from the train. "I'm not," said Stone; "they are."

"Good. You boys ought to get over to the gravel pit. Most everyone's still there. Some're burned pretty bad." Henly closed his eyes, shook his head. "There was little kids, just burning up in the street."

The gravel pit was a shallow cleft in the bare ground, filled with water on whose surface ash swayed like fabric. From the rim, Stone looked down at the people beginning to gather around the doctors. One man was milking a cow that stood knee-deep at the far end of the pool, filling watermelon rinds and passing them to children. Stone wrote in his notebook.

Beyond the gravel pit, he saw his first corpse. It lay on its back, bare except for its shoes. He couldn't tell the sex. The fire had shrunk it by perhaps a third, and tightened the muscles so that it lay in a boxer's position, facing death in tiny rage. A hundred feet away was another, and another, and then two more, who had died sheltering children.

There were more—perhaps twenty—where the depot must have been. The rails looped past them, bent into graceful arcs by the heat. Stone saw the ribs of a baggage wagon. A woman walked toward him, stepping obliviously over the dead, holding a baby to her breast.

"Ma'am!" She stopped, gave him a wide, empty look. Her hair was mostly gone. "Ma'am. The baby. It's—it's—" She covered it with her shawl and, still looking at Stone, sang, ". . . peace attend thee, all through the night. . . ."

"Ma'am." He held out his arms. "Perhaps you should give the child to me. It's—I'll see that Mr. Webber makes the—the proper arrangements."

She smiled at him and walked past singing. Stone wrote, "Woman with baby. Baby is . . ." He couldn't find a word. Finally he wrote, "adhesive."

He looked around. He was alone. He couldn't tell where the sun stood in the sky, but the day was heating up. Mirages jiggled in the dense, gleaming air. The empty morning hummed at him.

He got back to the gravel pit as fast as he could, found Webber and his gravediggers looking at corpses.

"Cemetery's that way," Webber said to his men. "Get the stretchers from the train. We'll start stacking them up. We'll be making a common grave." He glanced at the sky. "We'd better get them under pretty fast."

The gravediggers nodded. One pulled a pint bottle from his pants. Webber turned away.

People were coming out of the gravel pit now, squeezing water from their sleeves and trouser legs. Someone had got one of the milk cans over to the edge of the pit, and a small crowd of survivors had gathered around it. They dipped tin cups into the wide mouth and drank and chatted. One slopped milk on his shirt and laughed. Stone watched them. They all started laughing, men and women together, shaking their heads, moving their arms in wheeling, extravagant gestures, hugging their children, spilling milk.

By noon Stone, who hadn't really slept for a day and a half, was so tired he was giddy, but he had managed to piece together the events of the day before: the two trains, the flight to Skunk Lake, the hopeless stand of the firemen west of the town.

Chief Craig, gaunt and angry, showed him the wreckage of the new pumper. "Now," he said, "now maybe they'll all listen. Now maybe they'll give me the equipment I need."

"Would a bigger engine have made any difference?" Stone asked.

Craig looked down the hill. "There was the Brennan mill," he said, pointing to a dome of brown smoke, "and there was where Noble Barrett and the boys hit the log that came out of the forest—that was forest—and there's the man Father Lawler gave his last rites to."

The fireman looked down at the engine, its boiler peeled back to show a cluster of pipes.

"Naw," he said.

When Stone came off the hill with Craig, his weariness was such that he felt gusty moments of hilarity alternating with fierce anxiety. The small, lumpy corpses everywhere were by turns exciting fixtures that gave weight and focus to the day and dread reminders of the death that waited for him, for his wife, for the child she carried. All deaths were terrible.

They passed a photographer uncovering the cool eyes of his stereoscopic camera.

"Memorializing," Stone said aloud.

"What?" Craig asked.

"Nothing. What's all that?" They were by the tracks. The day was loud with the hammers of the men laying new rail along the riven St. Paul & Duluth right-of-way.

The track crews were setting down their hammers and going forward to help a group of men and women that was coming, stained and filthy, down the line.

Craig stuck his head forward. "I don't know where they're all coming from. Wait. That man—the one they're carrying—that's Jim Root!"

"Root," Stone said. "Oh! The engineer!"

Stone ran over, bumped some people aside. A burly black man and a fellow in city clothes stood holding a sagging old man whose hands were wrapped in grimy cloth.

"That Jim Root?" Stone asked. "I'm from the *Globe*."

The black man blinked at him. "This is James Root, the engineer on the limited. We are all in his debt."

Root mumbled something.

"What?" Stone asked.

"You—a—newspaperman?"

"Yes, sir."

"Tell them—I saved the locomotive."

"I surely will. Now you tell me how you did it."

Root moved his mouth, but nothing came out.

"Sir," the black man said, "the engineer is very ill."

"There's doctors by the gravel pit," Craig said. "Good work, Jim."

Root closed his eyes and Craig moved in on the man in city clothes, edged him out of the way, and, with the black man, carried off the engineer.

Stone nodded to the man in city clothes. His tie was gone and so were his eyebrows, but he looked pretty fit, despite it all.

"You don't come from these parts, do you?" Stone asked.

The man smiled at him. "God, but you look clean."

Stone shrugged, smiled back. "I wasn't in it."

"My name's Keegan. I'm a drummer for the Kraut and Dohnal Barber Supply Company of Chicago." He yawned, coughed, and rubbed his eyes. "Want to buy some barber supplies?"

Stone laughed.

"Neither does anybody else."

"So you were on the wonderful race of the limited?"

" 'Wonderful race.' You've already got the story down."

"I'm pretty tired." Stone stopped, embarrassed. "I mean, not like you, but forgive me if I'm talking funny."

Keegan waved the apology away. "It's fine. Yes, I was." He pointed at a pale, handsome woman with long dark hair and some sort of blanket wrapped around her waist. "She saved my life." The woman looked at Stone, saw his notebook, and walked away.

"How was that?"

"Just a moment." The drummer walked over to the woman. They spoke for a moment. She shook her head; Keegan patted her shoulder and returned to Stone.

"What I should tell you about is the lightning slinger." They walked away from the tracks while Keegan told of the young telegrapher who wouldn't quit his post. Stone wrote in his book. "What's his name?" he asked, when Keegan was done.

"Tom. I don't know his last name."

"I can find out. Now, what about you?"

"Well, I damned near got dead. I—" he stopped. "This where my hotel was? Yes. And over there was a son of a bitch of a barber. And there was a nice one about there, I guess."

With the buildings gone, the streets all seemed closer together. Hinckley looked as though it had been a mean little town.

"Yes," the salesman was saying, "and I left a sweet sample about there. Look!"

"Sample?" Stone asked, but Keegan was pawing through the rubble. "There." He held up a limp metal construction. "Quartersawn oak," he said ruefully, "very classy, but no good in a conflagration. That's a newspaper word, isn't it—conflagration?"

"I don't know what you're talking about."

The salesman gave him a dusty smile. "Sorry. I'm about played out. This used to be a miniature barber chair. Damn thing nearly killed me."

"How's that?"

Before Keegan could answer, a wagon came by carrying a dozen corpses. Stone took off his hat; Keegan didn't have one.

"How'd it almost kill you? The chair."

But Keegan had forgotten about the chair. He had crossed the street. "Look at this. This is where the hardware store was. Look." He kicked at something in the ash. "See?" Stone saw a spiny silver lump the size of a bread box. "Know what that was?"

"What?"

"Steel nails. The fire melted a barrel of steel nails. Know what this town is going to be needing?"

"What?"

"Hardware."

Stone giggled. The salesman looked hurt. "What's funny?"

"Well—I mean—" Stone couldn't stop laughing. "There's dead people everywhere, and no houses, and no railroad, and people hurt. I didn't mean to laugh. I just didn't expect to hear hardware, is all."

"I know hardware," Keegan said firmly, though he was swaying a little. "My father ran a hardware store. They're going to need it a hell of a lot more here than barber supplies."

"Course," said Stone. The man was off his head. Couldn't blame him, either.

"No, I mean a man could stay here and make a pretty good living on hardware."

"You want to *stay* here?"

The drummer reached up his arm and Stone, tired as he was, thought the man meant to hit him. He stepped back, then saw that Keegan just wanted to rub the back of his neck. He rubbed and kicked at the ground, then dropped his arm and looked squarely at Stone.

"Everyone was brave," he said.

Stone thought the ash was affecting his sight. Then he realized it was dusk. He had long since given up hoping for the day to end. The night, like the day, came from nowhere. The horizon grew dark all around at the same time, and a few minutes later the grayness overhead went, too. Trainmen pitched flares in the rubble, and soon the vanished town was brighter than it ever had been while it stood.

Hammers clanged in the dark. The line would be open tomorrow.

Stone had to get back tonight, had to get the story out. They still hadn't got a key working in Hinckley.

First, though, he had to find Webber.

He stopped a pair of stretcher-bearers. "Where's the graveyard?"

The man in front said, "Over there. Can't miss it. Liveliest place in town."

Stone walked across the tracks past the roundhouse to a hill ringed with torches. He heard planks being sawed.

Webber was standing near a trench, calling to the men inside it, "One more foot, then we're done for the night."

Stone tapped him on the shoulder. "How many?" he asked.

Webber's eyes were swollen and his face slack. "How many what?"

"Dead."

The two weary men stood a yard apart, facing each other, half dozing.

"There's some," Webber said after a while. He turned his thumb to a long mound. Stone had thought it was the dirt from the trench when he came up, but when he looked again he saw teeth in it. Arms stuck out from the top.

"How many there?"

"Ninety-six," said Webber.

"Ninety-six." Stone wrote in his book. "Think there'll be more?"

"More? Mister, they'll be coming in for days."

"How many?"

"Wouldn't guess. Three hundred, maybe four hundred."

"Damn."

"This lot, they're all going in the trench. We'll have coffins ready for the rest."

"That's good."

"They just found a bunch in the swamp a couple of miles north of here. They say that's where most of them died. They're already taking 'em out. Maybe you should go see."

Stone looked at the stack of corpses. They smelled like cooked food. It wasn't a bad smell, exactly, but if it hadn't been for the calm, strong odor of turned earth from the trench, he would have been sick for sure.

"No," he said. "No thank you, Mr. Webber. I don't think I'll go there."

He got out at midnight on a train going back for fresh supplies. He slept on the bed of a flatcar, and by the time he reached the newspaper office he'd lost his notebook. He sat at his desk almost weeping with frustration and exhaustion. But when he started to write, he found he remembered perfectly everything he'd seen, and all the names.

November 25

On Saturday, November 24, D.W. Cowan, the Pine County coroner, put his name to the official list of people who had died in the fire. The final entry read: "No. 413. Unknown—Male; nothing but bones and jack knife round; burned in mill yard."

The next morning, Scott Keegan sat in his windy yard. In a day or a week the wind would have knives in it, but now it blew softly, carrying the smell of the Lakes, barely disturbing his newspaper.

The newspaper was the Hinckley *Enterprise*, the first issue Angus Hay had gotten out since the fire. Keegan was sitting outdoors because he knew Hay would be by sooner or later, and he wanted to bait him.

Hay had written an editorial that began, "Fifteen years' work in fifteen minutes."

"That's a startling statement but true. In the language of the anthem, Northern Pine County has been 'twice refined.' The fire on September 1 did in fifteen minutes what it would have taken the husbandmen 75 years to accomplish. All nature is with us; it seemingly knew our needs, and came to clear the land.

"Come and see; no word can tell the opportunity afforded the farmer here since the fire. . . ."

Every small-town newspaper editor had to be a booster, and a booster was a salesman, and Keegan knew selling. Knew why Hay had written that callous rubbish. And looked forward to teasing Hay about it.

He didn't feel shy about teasing Hay. He'd taken half the back page of Hay's paper to advertise his hardware store, and had paid an extra dollar to have a linecut of a saw stuck in. It annoyed him to pay for a picture—people in Pine County knew what a saw looked like—but there was always the chance that some bastard would open another hardware store, and Keegan wanted his advertisement to be the flossiest.

The way you sold changed, depending on what you were selling. Keegan waited for Hay in denim pants; he'd left all his bright drummer's suits with a pawnbroker in Chicago. The weaselly man had given him twelve dollars for two hundred worth of fairly new clothes, but Keegan would have thrown them away otherwise, and he didn't mind. Here, nobody wanted fancy clothes. They wanted respectability. And so he looked out at the road across the first new picket fence in Hinckley. It was a different kind of selling.

He'd sold his first hardware—nails and hammers—out of a bin in a tent, a week after the fire. Now he had a real store. It was a hastily built shed, but well stocked, and in the spring he could put up a regular emporium. He even had help: a one eyed, prissy-talking bandit named Main, who knew a lot about bookkeeping.

A wagon rolled past on the road, its spokes lifting and dropping liquid mud like waterwheels. The driver gave him a wave, a little embarrassed, probably, to be working on a Sunday.

Keegan nodded. The driver lifted his hat. He was a man named Sprott who had been handling a dray in Hinckley since mid-October. He thought of Keegan as an original settler.

Keegan watched Sprott hie his horses down the street, then lifted the paper again.

The wind blew and blew and hammers ticked away. The state relief commission didn't stop on Sundays, either. Their men were still building houses for the survivors—sixteen by twenty-four feet for families, smaller for single people. Enough to give shelter when the winter came down.

Keegan had built his own house. It wasn't painted yet—it would be plain silly to use paint on your own house when you could clear ninety cents on the gallon on all you could get in—but it was big, and he'd built it without any relief funds from the commission. That was part of selling, too. You didn't open up a new territory on charity. Credit, yes—but not charity.

He looked at his advertisement. Maybe the saw was worth it, after all. It jumped right off the page at you.

"Twice refined," he said aloud. Where was Hay?

Betty came by first. They stood facing each other across the fence, talking about Thanksgiving. Her mother had survived in the gravel pit, and the state had built her a house. They'd never found a trace of her father.

Betty wanted Keegan to come there for the meal because it would mean a lot to her mother. He said he'd come only if he could supply the turkey.

"I have a brand-new stove, right in there." He pointed over his shoulder to his house. "Why doesn't she come over and cook on that? If it doesn't work, I'd like to know in time to exchange it."

Betty smiled. "Next year," she said.

They talked for a while. Keegan hadn't noticed Hay until he had already passed and was a good hundred feet down the road.

"Angus!" he yelled.

Hay turned around, put a hand to his ear.

Keegan glanced at Betty, regarding him calmly from across the fence. He waved the paper over his head and shouted, "Good work."

Afterword

"I presume the public will be surprised to hear from me at this late day," engineer William Best of the Eastern Minnesota wrote at the end of 1894, "but in justice to myself and others, I certainly think it is time for me to present a few facts . . . . From all that has been said and written of the adventurous trip of our train with the forest fires, on that day of horror, my railroad friends . . . must think that the train crew, as well as myself, were crazy. For instance, I have seen descriptions of how we ran over burning bridges at the rate of sixty miles an hour . . . . Why not say that I had engine 999 with a record of one hundred and twelve miles an hour; or that I slipped the wheels out from under engine No. 125 and substituted the Ferris Wheel, and all that I had to do was to touch the button and fly? Such fancies are suggested to me by the many exaggerated stories I have heard and read."

I have tried throughout this book to avoid exaggerating the event it describes, and that has not been particularly difficult; the fire that consumed Hinckley truly was cataclysmic, and the courage of the men and women who faced it truly extraordinary. (Best, who was as brave as anyone that day, devotes half a sentence to this uncommon heroism: ". . . their grit was good.")

Although I have not inflated or significantly altered events, the personalities I have ascribed to the leading characters are my own invention. For the most part, the names are real. They are a matter of record, but the record isn't very well known outside of eastern Minnesota, and I didn't want to change them. Scott Keegan, Pudgy LeMoyne, and Betty Langdon are entirely fictitious.

The Hinckley fire figures in many books and pamphlets, but the single major source remains *Memorials of the Minnesota Forest Fires*, a compilation of survivors' accounts and lists of relief benefactors brought out by the Reverend William Wilkinson the following year. The Reverend Wilkinson, perhaps realizing that he was unlikely ever again to have such a platform, takes the opportunity to include ancillary information of interest to him; the reader learns, for instance of "a sperm whale (phyester macrocephalus) appearing in the English Channel."

Two books that proved particularly illuminating about the era and the place were Trumen E. Moore's history of the drummer, *The Traveling Man*, and *We Made It Through the Winter*, Walter O'Meara's fine reminiscence of growing up in Cloquet, a lumber town a few miles up the line from Hinckley.

The town of Hinckley survives, but it has never managed to regain its old size. Today the population stands at around a thousand. The tracks still cross south of town, and the rebuilt St. Paul & Duluth depot still stands; it has become the Hinckley Fire Museum, which contains, among its other exhibits, a minutely detailed model of the town as it looked on the eve of its extinction, taped interviews with fire survivors, and a reconstruction of the telegraph bay where Tom Dunn gave his life.

A half mile east of the museum is the Hinckley cemetery, dominated by a handsome granite obelisk "dedicated to the pioneers of civilization in the forests of Minnesota." Behind it, they are more starkly commemorated by Webber's shallow troughs in the grass.